LAST LICKS!
WILL THE COXEMAN GET HIS?
AND IF HE DOES, WILL HE SURVIVE?

As a prominent sexologist, Rod Damon—The Coxeman—knew that often the pleasure of sex becomes so acute that it approaches pain.

But this was an untried theory until Rod was captured and tortured by a depraved band of beautiful enemy agents—part of an inhuman plot to rule the world.

Their erotic practices brought his mind and body to an almost unbearable pitch of agonizing ecstasy—a torture of unrelenting pleasure that he could not satisfy.

He had to escape their clutches to save his sanity, his sexual powers and the whole free world.

Wild?

Full of incredible surprises?

Yes! Yes! Now, read on! You won't stop till you come to the last line!

Other Books In This Series

by Troy Conway

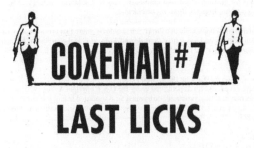

COXEMAN #7
LAST LICKS

AN ADULT NOVEL BY BY TROY CONWAY

POPULAR LIBRARY

Copyright © 1968 by Hachette Book Group USA
All rights reserved. Except as permitted under the U.S. Copyright Act of 1976, no part of this publication may be reproduced, distributed, or transmitted in any form or by any means, or stored in a database or retrieval system, without the prior written permission of the publisher.

Popular Library
Hachette Book Group USA
237 Park Avenue
New York, NY 10017

Popular Library is an imprint of Grand Central Publishing. The Popular Library name and logo is a trademark of Hachette Book Group USA, Inc. The Coxeman name and logo is a trademark of Hachette Book Group USA, Inc.

Visit our Web site at www.HachetteBookGroupUSA.com

First Printing: September, 1968

Cover photo by Paul Weller

Printed in the United States of America

Conway, Troy
Last Licks / Troy Conway
(Coxeman, #7)

ISBN 0-446-54313-6 / 978-0-446-54313-2

CHAPTER ONE

At first I thought sharks were attacking the woman.

I had seen her before, walking along the white sands of St. Tropez, which is a recently fashionable sector of the French Riviera and possesses the most attractive harbor on the entire coast. Always she wore gold lamé bikinis, from which her golden tan body flowed up and down in a series of soft, undulating curves.

Embarrassing as it is to say, I had tried to pick her up and had failed. Her dark brown eyes, which could have been so warm and melting, had been pools of dirty ice, cutting me cold. Her long, flowing brown hair had flicked the air with indignation when she gave a pert toss to her head, erasing me completely from the scene.

But now she was in trouble.

I was sculling about the waters off the fashionable Epiplage beach, just exercising my muscles, trying to keep in shape even though I was on vacation, when I heard her scream. My eyes bulged a little. I had been watching her smooth crawl stroke, trying to think up a better means of approach, when suddenly she gave a nervous squawk and disappeared from view.

A shark has her leg! I thought.

I rose to my feet and dived, all in one fast movement. I had no knife, I lacked any kind of weapon—after all, I was on vacation, here along the Côte des Maures—but I had some vague notion that if I splashed around a lot I could rescue my bronzed bathing beauty from the jagged teeth of a whale shark.

I hit the blue waters and went down in a long slide.

5

Ahead of me, I could make out the woman, floundering and trying to fight in the hands of two men. Even as I shot toward them, I found my eyes searching for their scuba equipment, for the sight of an oxygen tank or a mouthpiece.

There were none. The men had only tiny black mini-briefs the same as myself, about their loins. They were lean, hard fellows, and they were just about to strangle my unknown lady.

I came in straight for the man on the left.

My name is Rod Damon. I am a Coxeman, a member of the Thaddeus X. Coxe Foundation, which in turn is an organization of secret agents whose task it is to do the dirty work around the world in the interests of American democracy and international peace. As a Coxeman, I have become extremely proficient in the arts of karate and judo. I have made my body into a living weapon. I felt quite confident when I saw my two opponents.

The man on the right had a strangle hold on the woman with his forearm. I could see her hands pawing weakly at that flesh-bar choking out her life as the man on the left turned and came for me.

I did a backflip in the water, I rammed my foot against his jaw. I drove him back, but he was tough. He came in for me from below. His intention, I believe, was to clasp my legs and drag me down.

My lungs were straining at this point. I needed air.

Apparently these underwater swimmers did not.

Muscular arms were wide apart to clasp me when I flutterkicked with my feet and rammed my head into the man windpipe-wrecking the bronze lady. I felt him grunt and turn a little. My hand was shooting upward as fast as I could send it, the fingers formed into a cone and driving for the right side of his throat, just under the jaw. This is a human weak point. Had we been in open air—and had my blow connected—he would have been off the scene, but the water slowed me down. The man dodged the blow just enough to deflect it from its target so that I hit him in the throat itself. But he was forced to let go of the woman to do this.

She started toward the surface, swimming frantically.

I tried to follow, but the man below me had a grip on one leg now, and was letting his weight go dead. He was like an anchor dragging me bottomward. I felt ready to explode. My lungs were collapsing from the need for air. My vision was blurring.

I expected the strangler to come at me too. Between them I wouldn't have stood the chance of a snowman in Hell. I doubled up in the arms of the man who had tackled me, and put both my thumbs on his eyes.

Sure, dirty pool. But my life was at stake.

I got no chance to gouge out his eyes. His arms let me go. I gave him a kick in the back of the head as I went up like an Apollo missile out of Cape Kennedy. Moments later I was gasping for some warm Mediterranean air and floundering like a beached fish.

The bronze lady was going up over the moldboard of my narrow boat, curving legs kicking, her smooth white buttocks half out of the abbreviated bikini loincloth. Then hands were on my ankles, yanking me downward.

I drew in a lungful of Riviera air.

I was mad by this time. And scared, as well.

What kind of men was I fighting? They didn't need scuba equipment to breathe—apparently didn't need to breathe at all under water. Were they some kind of outer space creatures who looked like men? Were they from some underwater Atlantis, submerged thousands of years before and by now acclimated to living beneath the surface of the sea?

I had to act fast, before they did me in. All they had to do—since they could breathe in these watery depths and I couldn't—was hold me until I drowned. By that time my unknown tanned tomato might be safe on Epi-plage beach, but I would be a dead Damon.

I like life too much to let that happen, so I bent and fastened my fingers in the neck of the nearest swimmer and tightened them like a vise in throatflesh. He started kicking and struggling, and his hands came up to my wrists and tried to pry me loose.

I knew one thing for sure then. He had to breathe.

7

Somehow he was able to extract oxygen from the water as a fish does, so he didn't need any apparatus to stay beneath the surface for long periods of time. My fingers locked in place, I kicked back at his companion at the same time, getting his nose with my heel.

I swam upward with my hands on a throat. I held that throat, I ignored the pain of fingers scrabbling across my face while searching for my eyes. I saw a dark shadow right above me and headed toward it.

With all my strength, I lifted his head toward the keel of my shallow boat. Even underwater, the hollow thunk made a heartwarming sound. I indulged my heart. I hammered his head five times against the wooden keel until his every muscle was limp.

I let his body sink downward, lazily drifting through the clear water while I grabbed the moldboard and hoisted myself upward for another gulp of air. I saw the woman in the golden bikini staring at me with wide eyes, crouched forward.

I winked. "Relax, honey. One down, one to go."

I let go and sank, just in time. The other merman was coming for me with a chunk of jagged rock in his right hand. I swam backward and down, kicking up with a foot. I landed right on his genitals. He shuddered and doubled up, letting go the stone.

I dived under him and grabbed the rock. It was sharp, it damn near cut my hand when I wrapped my digits around it. The hell with a few cuts! I swam upward behind my victim.

He was still doubled over, so I wrapped my legs about his back and hammered his skull with the rock, again and again. I kept right on doing that until my need for air was greater than my desire to crack his head wide open.

I let him go and moved surfaceward.

My shallow-draft scull was maybe ten feet away. The bronze lady was still crouched in it, her eyes scanning the water, off to one side. She did not see me until I put a hand on the boat. Then she whirled, crying out in alarm.

"Easy, easy," I grinned, lifting myself into the boat.

"Toll!" she exclaimed in excellent German. "Did you

8

really defeat them? It cannot be! Impossible!"

"Honey, nothing is impossible to the president, founder and chief field worker of the League for Sexual Dynamics."

Those honey-brown eyes widened as an imp of laughter brightened them. Their lashes were long; they added to the overall loveliness of the heavily tanned face with the long brown hair hanging on either side.

"*Ach*, so? An *Amerikaner*?" The full red lips moved into a smile. "You are the fresh one who has been ogling my body for the past three days, *nein*?"

"I'm afraid so, ma'am," I admitted, reaching for the oars. "My parents instilled a love of beauty in me while they were bringing me up, and you're the most beautiful thing I've seen since I arrived!"

Her laughter was deep, sensual. Being a woman, she could not resist letting me see just how beautiful she was, by stretching her arms up over her head, exposing her shaven armpits and most of her extremely voluptuous body. Her breasts pulled out of the bra almost completely, so I saw the upper arc of her nipples, while her belly flattened out to the beginning curve of her mons veneris. Her thighs were tanned from the sun and looked like dark whipped cream.

Her laughter choked off quickly as a look of alarm touched her features and she turned her head to scan the water. She had a great profile, full mouth and dimpled chin, with a broad forehead and perfect nose.

"What about—them?" she asked.

"They aren't in any condition to come visiting," I reassured her, sliding the oarblades into place, cutting deep into the water, feathering them for a return stroke.

"You do not know them," she muttered.

"But you do?"

Her eyes stabbed at me, alert, suspicious. For a long moment she hesitated, then nodded. "*Ja, ja*. I know them. They are mermen."

"I figured that out for myself. They breathe the same way a fish does. They don't have to come up for air. They can extract it from the water itself."

She scowled prettily, still nervously glancing back and

9

forth over the limpid blue water. "Yes, you know. That much, at least."

"What I don't know is, how come?"

"How come?" she puzzled over the colloquialism.

"Why did they do it?"

Her face cleared, and she smiled. "Oh. Yes, I understand."

"But you're not talking."

She turned and looked behind us at the distant beach which was becoming more distant with every stroke of my oars. Her heavy lips smiled faintly as she turned back to me. "You're going in the wrong direction," she pointed out.

I shook my head. "No, I rented this scull to get some exercise, and I mean to get it, no matter what humdrum happenings in our everyday world interrupt."

"You are mad," she exclaimed; then added, "like all Amerikaner."

"Maybe. I was just wondering why those mermen wanted to kill you. It seems such a waste of beauty."

She leaned over to trail her fingers in the water. The action lifted her big breasts in the bra cups. They were not tanned as was the rest of her lush flesh; they were white, with faint blue veins, and they formed soft globes with a deep vale between them.

"I may not tell you that," she murmured.

"Fair enough," I nodded. "Then just be quiet, sit back, and enjoy the ride. I've been loafing for the past week, traveling here. I really do need to tone up my muscles."

Her eyes assessed my chest, moving across my shoulders and along my arms, and studying the washboard musculature of my torso before settling on the black minibriefs that did not quite contain my manhood. She stared steadily for long moments, but the mini still bulged. She did not know, of course, about my priapism, the state of being perpetually erect.

She lifted a cupped hand and leaning forward, splashed my minimum with the cooling water. "There, there. Your muscles appear to be in excellent shape—but this isn't the time to use them."

10

Her hand went on giving me cold baths while her body tried to keep me interested, because every time she leaned forward, her thighs opened to display the crease in her gold lamé bikini pants and her breasts almost spilled out into the open. She seemed very intent on her work; she never took her eyes off it. Under the bra cups, I saw that her nipples were quite stiff.

After a while she leaned back and asked softly, "What did you say you were president of?"

"L.S.D. The League for Sexual Dynamics. I teach the young and sometimes the not so young all about sex and its many diversifications." I eased the oars out of the water and let the bateau glide.

"It is very rewarding work," I explained, watching her reach behind her with her arms and clasp the moldboards, moving her shoulders a little so her soft breasts jellied. "I make sure the young realize how happy their lives can be by properly understanding the pleasure their bodies can give them. I open the formerly locked doors to my older clients, so that they may realize what they have been missing."

"A carnal crusader, a diddling do-gooder," she murmured.

"In a sense, I suppose you can say that. It has become a very important adjunct to my sociology work. When my students leave, they are better fitted for life outside the university halls, believe me."

"You seem unusually well-equipped to do such work," she said, glancing boldly at my briefs. "And you can fight too." Her eyes were curious. "Why is that? Most professors I know are doddering old scholars or scrawny young idealists. What makes you so different?"

"A healthy mind in a sound body, sans mens, sans corpore, as the Romans say it. You have to be healthy to enjoy sex. That's a basic fundamental. So I keep healthy by eating good food, plenty of fresh air and exercise, and all that advertising jazz."

"I feel as if I'm back in school."

"You might enjoy my course, at that."

Her eyes mocked me, so I dipped the blades into the

11

water and began rowing again. We were silent, the bronzed lady staring out to sea, my own eyes caught between her exposed flesh and her lovely face, and the sight of the yachts riding at anchor in the harbor more than a mile away.

St. Tropez is a tiny little fishing village that has become world famous only in the past decade. It is part of the French Riviera, but it does not cater to visitors the way Cannes and Monaco and Portofino do. There is one road in or out of town, and there are accomodations for maybe two thousand people, no more. It is the playground for such French movie stars as Brigitte Bardot and Juliette Mayniel, for directors like Roger Vadim and Claude Chambrol. It is avant-garde, it is groovy, it is *the* place to be.

There is no golf, no tennis, no gambling salon. There are the fishing boats—if you are with it, the crusty *pecheurs* will take you along when they put you out to sea—and the palatial yachts, the several beaches like Epi-plage and Tahiti, a couple of hotels and some shops.

There is also the hot sunlight and the cool water.

For a rest spot, it was ideal in my eyes, because as a professor of sociology I enjoy studying the social mores of the boys and girls, men and women, who swing our world. I do not study their actions from the bound volumes of newspapers or magazines. When I can, I like to get turned on with them and become a real day-tripper.

Like now, with this nearly naked woman.

"Might I invite you to a *coquetelle* at Bertoncini's?" I asked my companion, turning the scull toward the beach. "After you have showered?"

"I thought you'd never ask," she smiled. "Permit me to introduce myself. I am the Baroness Zia von Osterreich." Her tanned shoulders shrugged, as she added, "A meaningless title, an unknown name these days, but when de Maupassant and Matisse came here, the title and the name were very important."

I took it I was accepted. It is not an easy thing to be accepted in Saint Tropez. It is a closed corporation, very clannish, very indifferent to most outsiders. I felt that Zia von Osterreich had been coming to Saint Tropez a long

12

time, and that if she vouched for me, my stay here was going to a hoot.

She murmured, "I really must thank you for saving my life. You shouldn't have been able to do so—against the mermen—yet you did."

"Tell me, who or what are these mermen?"

A pink fingernail traced an unknown symbol on her thigh. Her eyes were downcast, watching what she did. Suddenly she shot a glance at me from under her long brown lashes, and just as suddenly she burst into laughter.

"You look like a poker player. Are you? This sign I've made"—her hand indicated her thigh "—you don't know what it means, do you? Or are you familiar with it and won't tell me?"

She had been doing some thinking, the baroness had. Maybe she thought I was one of the mermen, from the way I had polished them off.

"Do you?" I asked suddenly. "Do you think I'm one of them? Is that what's in your head? You're trying to find out something, I know."

She giggled suddenly, as if delighted. "No, no. You are not a merman. This much I know, at least. But that you might be . . . somebody interested in them; this I do think."

"Well, I'm not."

I ran the scull up onto the white sand and turned to help Zia von Osterreich from the boat. She let me hold her hand a moment as she lifted a long bare leg and came over the moldboard to the wet sand. Then she seemed to stumble slightly and fell against me.

The touch of her big breasts and bare belly to mine touched off the explosive fury of my manhood. I grew up to full stature against her bikini pants. Her eyes narrowed to sensuous slits as she pressed herself into me.

"*C'est par la*, that's why," she murmured in perfect French.

"What's why?" I asked stupidly.

Her laughter rang out as she nudged my swollen sex with her gold laméd front. "*Cela!* Your maleness."

I must have looked ridiculous with my mouth hanging open, but she put a soft fingertip on my lips and ran it

13

around gently. There was an odd tenderness in her gesture. "The coquetelle, eh? At Bertoncini's?"

I picked up the blue and white Pan-American satchel that had been given me as a first-class passenger on the big Boeing jetliner which had deposited me in France. I kept my wallet, the keys to the Alfa Romeo I'd hired in Marseilles, and my passport, inside it. My shirt and sandals were on the blanket where I'd left them to go sculling. A boy came running to retrieve the boat. I flipped him a twenty-franc piece. He would row the bateau back to its quay.

I walked beside the baroness to her own blanket, where she bent to pick up a white shirt and slide her arms into it. She knotted it three inches above her navel. She put her feet in wooden clogs and was dressed for going anywhere in Saint Tropez. There is no formality in this little fishing village.

I was dressed when I put on my own shirt and sandals.

We moved thigh to thigh along the white sand toward my Alfa Romeo. In the distance I could see the naked bodies of the sun worshippers who made a brief stretch of the Epi-plage into a nudist colony. Everything is free and easy here in this hot sunlight. The baroness giggled as she saw me staring, and suggested that tomorrow we join the *nues*.

We drove to Bertoncini's wineshop. There were a score of little tables there, surrounded by chairs. We had to push our way into the shop through men and women who were so obviously tourists it hurt to see them. A bare arm lifted and waved. Zia cried out at sight of it and used me to run interference. We were soon shoved against a table where there was a single empty chair. I sat down and I pulled her onto my lap.

She gave me a surprised look then laughed. "I should have known such a one would have known the answer to the problem." Then she turned to her friends, saying, "This is Rod—no dirty remarks, Claudine!—who just saved my life."

She told the story amid exclamations of delight and fright from the artists and their women crowded in around our table. Somebody came and put two coquetelles before us. I sipped at mine while Zia wriggled her behind around

14

on me. I think she delighted in stirring me up.

I was the fair-haired boy-hero after she finished her tale. Her friends—I caught the names Gaby, Pierre, Marina, Ange, Serafin and Claudine—insisted on standing treat, and one or two of the girls leaned across the tabletop to give me open-mouthed kisses in gratitude for the fact that I had brought Zia safely back to shore.

One fact about the recital I had noticed as Zia related it. There had been no mention of mermen. Instead, I had saved her from a shark that had somehow found its way in close to the beach. According to her story, I'd had a knife in my travel bag; I had used it to kill the shark that had been last seen drifting toward the bottom with my knife still in it.

We talked about sharks for a while. Cousteau had made a movie about them, he had mentioned them in his books, and these people had read him very thoroughly. They knew as much about them as any marine biologist. They also mentioned the fact that sharks were almost unknown in the Mediterranean.

"A loner," I contributed.

"*Oui*," murmured the baroness, glancing at me slowly, "an underwater Jack the Ripper."

We talked about Jack the Ripper.

Then Zia got off my middle and stretched, saying, "It's time I had my shower. Rod and I are going to the Esquinade."

This was news to me, but I was all for it. I told everybody I had to go take a shower too—unfortunately not with Zia (at which they all laughed)—and be ready for my big date. We walked off hand in hand with our bare thighs brushing.

The baroness told me she owned a little house some miles outside town, not far from the hill village of Ramatuelle. She had ridden a bicycle into town, but she would make better time back and forth if she borrowed my Alfa Romeo. I stood on the cobbled street and watched her drive off, barely missing a middle-aged man in the red and white uniform of a *bravado*.

In my room at the Hotel de la Tour, I slid out of my shirt

15

and swimtrunks, poured myself a glass of red wine, and contemplated my navel. During the past year or two, ever since I have been a Coxeman working with the Thaddeus X. Coxe Foundation, I have been discovering a new side to myself. Formerly I was content to be a university professor and founder of the League for Sexual Dynamics. Walrus-moustache, my case officer for the Foundation, changed all that.

He made me a secret agent. He also turned me into a living radar unit, continually tuning my instincts in on intrigue. I knew damn well Walrus-moustache would want to know about these mermen who could swim underwater for indeterminate lengths of time, who could get the oxygen their bodies needed from the water itself. I admitted I would like to know more myself.

So I spent a few bucks and telephoned the United States.

It was not all that fast. I put in my call, I walked into my shower and frothed up a lather. I stood and let the cold water drum down on my manhood as it clamored for attention whenever I thought about the baroness. It took a lot of cold water, but I was relatively calm and half dressed—in skintight pants and sandals and a clean shirt—when the telephone shrilled.

"Hello, hello?" I asked.

"Who's this?" a faint voice answered.

"Your special agent, Chief—your man in Saint Tropez."

"I thought you were on a vacation."

"I am. But something's come up——"

"Not again! Stop bragging."

"That isn't what I mean."

I clued him in on the mermen.

There was a little silence, then he said, "Hold the fort, Professor. I'm coming. I want to learn more about these mermen from the lady herself."

"She may not talk."

A dirty chuckle was my answer.

"So okay," I agreed. "I have ways, but you're going to let me do it on my own. Neither the lady nor I like audiences, I think."

16

"All right. Find out what you can. I'll be there in a day or two. And, Damon—be careful."

"Your concern has me all hung up."

"If those men tried to kill the baroness, they may succeed in killing you. Be warned."

"I'm warned. So for now, *au revoir*."

I hung up and walked downstairs and out onto the promenade. I had not long to wait before my Alfa Romeo braked to a stop before me. The baroness was at the wheel, her dark brown hair piled up like a crown on her head in an upsweep with tiny pearls winking through it.

"*Bonjour*," she caroled.

I hopped in, seeing that she was wearing a micro-skirt and black patterned stockings, with a frilly shirtwaist that was as transparent as mist. I could even make out the dark areolas of her large brown nipples. She looked like a tourist lady. She laughed when I told her so.

"I thought you might enjoy seeing me like this."

She had excellent legs and the patterned hose made them very modish. She could have been an American jet-setter. I was hardly in the seat than she was off with a screech of tires on the cobbles.

"We are not going to the Esquinade," she informed me, eyes ahead to watch the road. "I have another cave cafe in mind. The Diabolique. You'll like it." Her eyes slid from the road to my face for a moment.

"I do admit being in a hell-raising mood," I commented.

Her soft chuckle was a compliment to my wit. She drove easily and with a competent manner that made me wonder if she would be as skillful in a bed. I intended to find out before the night was too far advanced.

The Diabolique was one of those entertainment spots like the Esquinade and the Tropicana. There was an oaken door set in what looked like a ordinary hill. Twin torches flared on either side, illuminating the carved face of the devil himself, carved in rock above the door. There was a parking lot to one side of the hill. A uniformed boy came running as the baroness braked.

We moved toward the oak door.

17

An instant before we touched it, the door swung open. Electric eye beam? I wondered. Then I saw a girl devil in tight red nylon pantihose, with bare breasts shoving out invitingly at us, her pretty face masked in a scarlet domino. She wore a devil-cap with pointed ears above the mask.

"Madam, monsieur," she whispered.

The baroness patted the girl's right breast. I figured it might be some kind of password, so I patted the other one. The girl giggled and wriggled a little as we caught her nipples and tugged gently on them.

"*Ca chatouille*," she protested. "That tickles!"

"We may see you later, Violane," Zia murmured. Turning to me, she asked, "You enjoy a troilism occasionally, *non*?"

"Occasionally, yes," I nodded, and catching Violane, I kissed her bare shoulder, pressing myself against her scarlet behind and finding it soft and yielding.

"He is *tres fou*," the girl shrieked, doubling up with laughter, managing to back herself still harder into me.

"He's an Amerloque," commented Zia, as if my being American explained everything. "But he's a nice Amerloque."

"A nice Amerloque," murmured Violane reflectively, continuing to sample my size with her buttocks.

Zia caught my hand. "Come, darling. Don't pay any attention to the little tart. She's only agitating for a tip."

I let myself be drawn along by the hand but I slipped out a hundred-franc note, folded it and sailed it through the air at the girl-devil. She caught it and blew me a kiss between giggles.

There was a worn stone staircase before us, lighted by a row of red-flaring torches. If I didn't know better, I would have said this was one of the entryways to Hell itself. There was a sign in French reading, "Abandon Hope, All Ye Who Enter Here." Just like the real thing.

A man in a devil costume, complete with tail and trident, stood before a door heavy with erotic carvings. I would have paused to study them—with my role as president of L.S.D. in mind—but Zia tugged at me.

"*Entrez, entrez*," she cried.

18

I followed her through the door.

Out of the shadows to the right another devil came leaping. He appeared so suddenly I had no time to stop him. He held a naked knife in his hand. With a bloodcurdling scream, he plunged the steel shaft into Zia von Osterreich's soft belly.

The blade went deep, out of sight.

CHAPTER TWO

I stood frozen in utter horror.

Then my nerves unwound and I catapulted forward, my right hand rigid, chopping down at the scarlet neck of the red-clad killer. For a moment I was insane with fury.

Zia screeched, *"Gott in Himmel! Nein! Nein!"*

I tried to stop the blow but the edge of my hand landed and the devil went flying across the floor to land up against a table containing a small fortune in trays and glassware. The table skidded and splintered. The glasses went flying, shattering and breaking all over the place.

Half a hundred diners and drinkers froze into shocked silence.

I was standing at the balustraded entrance into what looked like a grotto out of Hell. The walls were gray stone, and were hung with the pitchforks generally associated with Beelzebub, also with glossy photographs of naked men and women in varied love poses. Some of them were mural size. There was a bar in the far distance, where devils served as bartenders. Half a dozen girls in black kitten costumes—witches' familiars—were serving drinks on trays.

Everybody stopped and stared.

Zia was screaming. "It is the joke, the scare thing. *Mein Gott!* You have already kill two men today. 'Ow many you want to kill?"

When she got excited, Zia forgot her precise English. I stared at her unmarked belly, at the knife with the retractable blade that lay on the floor, at the inert man in the devil costume lying amid the splintered ruins of the table.

20

"Sorry about that, Zia," I mumbled.

A roar of delight exploded in the room. Knives clanged against glasses in a symphony of sympathetic understanding. A man in evening clothes came hurrying through the din, his face white.

"Your highness! Baroness!" he pleaded. "What is it?"

I bent and picked up the knife. I touched its dull point. The blade slid back into the long handle. I went red with embarrassment. Zia spread her hands as she looked around the room. She loved audiences, I decided.

"This man is an Amerloque," she began. "This afternoon he saved my life from a shark. It is getting to be a habit."

The room roared with pleasure. This was something new, a little *lagniape* to break the monotony of small-talk and familiar drinks. I caught a few phrases here and there.

"Teach the beggar not to pull those stunts!"

"I wish you'd done that, Henry!"

"*Mon Dieu!* I think he killed Raoul. Somebody go see."

"Baroness, trust you to find Tarzan in Saint Trop!"

The man in the tuxedo was flowing with apologies. I offered to pay for the damage, but he would not hear of it. It was worth it in entertainment value, M. Ambert assured me. Himself out in front, he escorted us to a table. I threw a look back over my shoulder. Raoul was coming to, being assisted to his feet by the devil-clad doorman and two black kittens.

Zia said, "I need a double brandy after that, M'sieu Ambert."

"Make it two," I echoed.

M. Ambert hovered above us, still murmuring his apologies, interspersing his words with Gallic gestures to a kitten and a barman. "Not for the world would I have had this happen, your highness. Not for two worlds! Ha-ha! It is most unfortunate that you are so embarrassed."

Zia was not embarrassed. She was preening herself, smiling at grinning faces, winking and making moués of her full red mouth as she blew kisses or gurgled happy laughter at the women. The thought touched me that had she wanted me to stay out of the action, she would have

21

warned me what might be coming, and not to be startled.

The minx had wanted to see my reactions!

I put a hand under the scarlet tablecloth, reached up under her skirt to her soft inner thigh and pinched. Zia lurched and gave a mock scream.

"Darling, control yourself! This is not the place."

"If we're in hell, I'm going to be a devil," I shouted.

This drew a round of applause. Mr. Ambert beamed. Our black kitten waitress was beside me, holding her breath, her green eyes wary behind her cat mask. This black nylon kitten costume was very cleverly fashioned. Two holes in front permitted her bare breasts to protrude, so that they shook and jumped as she moved. A black netting stretching from her navel to her upper thighs all but exposed her shaven femininity. And from behind, as I was soon to discover. . . .

The kitten bent to hear what Zia wanted. This presented a fluffy cat's tail to my inquisitive hand. I reached out, caught hold of it and lifted. The girl whooped and bucked. I found myself staring at a stark naked behind, very plump, very attractive.

M. Ambert exclaimed, "Where did you find this one, highness?"

The uproar in the cave casino was hitting about a hundred decibels. My ears ached with the noise. In the background, men and women were standing at their tables, the better to see what the mad American might be doing. Zia was giggling fit to kill, while the kitten was staring at me with less fear and with something like invitation in her green eyes.

"My uncle was an explorer," I told the room.

Our nearest neighbors asked M. Ambert where he had hired the new performer. He denied it, spreading his hands and swearing upon *le bon Dieu* that I was a mere visitor, a friend of her highness the baroness. And her highness agreed, explaining once again how I had knifed a shark to death in the waters beyond the harbor this very afternoon.

A woman in a low-cut evening gown, her shoulders and breasts all but bare, leaned over and pressed her hand to

22

my upper arm. "Your must be very strong. Let me feel your muscles."

I bent my arm for her obediently. She gripped my muscle but her sly eyes told me she would much rather be gripping something else. I leaned forward to kiss her soft throat.

Zia had paused in her recital of my heroism to listen. So I obliged her by whispering into the perfumed ear with the diamond earring just above my lips, loudly enough for everyone to hear, "*Ou est la chambre a coucher?* The bedroom, honey—where's it at?"

Zia kicked upward between my legs. Fortunately, she missed. "Not before the soup, you barbarian!"

Everybody thought that was Comedie Française stuff.

By this time our kitten was back with our double brandies and was standing right next to me; in hope I'd give her tail another yank, I think. But as president of the League for Sexual Dynamics, I have always adhered to my own motto: In fight or frolic, always keep them off balance.

So I caught her by her slim middle, drew her toward me, and kissed both her bright red nipples. She gasped, Zia gasped, they all gasped. Then I drew out a hundred-franc note, turned her around, lifted her cat's tail and wedged it in place.

There was a burst of applause. Zia glared daggers.

I hunched my chair close to hers, and said in a stage whisper, "*Vous avez un de ces corps, c'est incroyable!* Your shape is absolutely unbelievable! *Certainment, que c'est du chique!* Certainly it can't be natural!"

"Buffoon!" Zia snarled.

The people were laughing. M. Ambert was beaming. Zia was mad.

I lifted my brandy glass, swirled its golden contents, and sipped. I knew she kept glancing at me stormily as she pretended to stare haughtily about the room. It was my cue to woo her, to make her understand that the kitten and the lady in the evening gown were mere incidentals.

"You see, I was nervous," I explained.

"*Hein?*" she exclaimed, startled.

"Ever since I was alone with you in the boat this afternoon, I have been in a state of perpetual excitement. I took

23

three cold showers, but it didn't help. You are the most desirable woman I have ever known. As a result, I am nervous near you. I don't know how long my self-control can last."

"Hah!"

No woman alive can resist flattery like *that*. She sniffed and stared off into space, but the lips that had thinned with anger were relaxing into their familiar, sensual pout. For a moment I thought the evening was going to be a fiasco, but she turned a flushed face to me, and after a hesitant moment, she began to speak.

"If you are telling the truth, I would be the happiest woman in France, but I know you are a buffoon, you are a comedian. You will do anything for a laugh. You are probably laughing at me right now."

I caught her hand and drew it to my lap. It pressed into me firmly for a long instant, then withdrew. Her cheeks were flushed, even in the candlelight, and her eyes were brilliant behind the long brown lashes.

"That's no laughing matter," I told her.

"The sight of that kitten's *derrière* made it that way."

"The kitten wasn't around in the boat."

She remembered all right. She sighed and let a fingernail march across the tabletop. "Perhaps I shall make you prove what you said . . . later."

I was fishing around for an answer to that when the black curtain behind us started to swish back. A red light came out into the candlelit room. I turned my head casually, and stiffened.

I was staring at a stage made up to look like a bedroom in hell. There was a big easy chair at the left of the stage, a straight-backed spindle chair next, a huge bed seemingly carved out of ebony and gold, and finally a piano and a long, narrow bench. A handsome, blonde young man sat at the piano, playing softly.

A sigh went about the room. Chair legs scraped as they were turned so the audience might see the stage from anywhere in the room. There are four such stages in the Diabolique. No one knows which stage is to be used on any given night, so nobody can decide where they want to sit for the best view. Unless, of course, M. Ambert seats them close as a mark of favor—as he may or may not have done with the baroness.

A sepulchral voice spoke offstage.

"You are damned, Danielle Richefeu. You must pay the penalty to his Satanic Majesty, forever throughout eternity!"

Now you could hear a woman sobbing. It was very realistic, and you really seemed to be looking on into some lost corner of Hell. After a moment you heard a female voice.

"Please, no. I haven't sinned that much! Please, let me go. I will do anything."

"Exactly. It is why you are here. You'll do . . . anything."

"Please! Please, I beg you——"

The sepulchral voice grew crafty. "There is a way. We have been honored this night by an attendance of future victims of hellfire"—nervous titters and laughter from the people in the audience at that—"and it has come to me that if you can win a reprieve from them, I shall send you back to Earth to live out the rest of your days."

"Yes. Yes. I agree. I do, I agree."

There was a silence, then the sound of dragging footsteps. From the right, where the blonde young man played the piano, a girl came into view. When she saw the young man, she gasped and turned away, hiding her face with her hands.

"Yes, that is Paul, your piano teacher."

The girl turned and stared at the audience. She was wearing a child's dress that was all frills and lace, belted with a white satin sash. She had a matching bow in her long blonde hair. The audience knew this was no child, but she was so costumed and was such an excellent actress, that they began to believe it.

"Must I?" she whimpered.

"If you would go back," said the mournful voice.

She was a pretty little thing, there was panic on her grotesquely twisted mouth and in her wide blue eyes. Her legs beneath the micro-shirt were amply curved and rather

25

exciting, all pale white flesh above the Baby Jane shoes and small white socks. She really did seem to be only twelve years old.

She ran to the piano bench, her hands reached out. In an instant, she was playing a duet with the handsome young man. They played very well together.

"Paul, I saw you the other day—with *Maman*," she murmured suddenly.

"Did you, Danielle?"

"*Oui*. She was doing something to you. . . ."

The little girl swallowed hard and hung her head. The blonde youth turned his face to her. Their hands slid from the keys. His hand touched her blonde hair and ran down it to fondle her soft neck.

"And?" he prompted.

She cast one terrified glance at the audience, then swung to face the piano teacher. She appeared to gather courage as his hand went up and down her back.

"I shall tell Papa—unless you let me."

The young man started, then whispered, "You are black-mailing me, little one. But—very well, I agree."

Danielle gave a happy little cry and put her hand on her companion. His body shuddered in reaction. His eyes watched her little hand grasp the zipper and run it down. Then he cried out sharply as her hand disappeared from sight. They had swung around, so that his front faced the tables. Everyone could see the hand moving under his trousers, everyone could hear the shrill cries of excitement and watch her bare legs move together.

Then everyone saw her hand emerge, gripping its prey.

"Paul, Paul," she babbled, staring down.

"Easy, little one," he panted.

She let her head droop, until she could press her cheeks against him. She turned her head so her blonde hair pressed into his belly, and she began to kiss him. The audience was staring, some of the women were making low, moaning noises. Everyone could see very plainly what was taking place. Her hand gripped, her lips caressed. The young man began to shudder.

His hands shoved her around and down between his

26

thighs. I could hear a woman laugh harshly, somewhere behind me. The candles on each table flared; this was the only light outside the crimson glow of the room in Hell.

The girl was kneeling before her piano teacher, head burrowing into him. The young man had his head thrown back, he was making groaning sounds with his throat. Then he bent forward, spasmodically, and his fingers grabbed hold of her white lace dress. They began lifting it upward.

The girl had nothing on under the short dress. Her pale buttocks made twin moons above her full thighs, quivering as her head lifted and fell. Slowly those thighs parted, until a golden puff could be seen. The young man bent his head far forward, staring, but he did not hide anything from the view of the audience.

The climax was coming swiftly. The young pianist was gasping, his hips were stabbing, his hands slid down to bury their fingers in the soft buttockflesh. Then when he cried out thickly, his hands went inside the bare thighs, lifting and spreading them.

The girl was raised up off the floor, completely visible.

They froze that way for long minutes.

The stage went dark.

The sepulchral voice intoned, "This was the beginning, Danielle. Can you deny it?"

"No! No! I don't deny it. But I was so young—scarcely twelve. I didn't know what I was doing." There was a pause, then she whimpered, "Ask the audience."

The audience applauded until the cave cafe rang. A few male voices cried, "Bravo, Bravo." Here and there a thickened female voice chimed in with its vocal approval.

The deep voice said sarcastically, "Apparently my domain will have to find *liebensraum* to accomodate all those who belong here."

A cheer went up from the tables.

The red light began to glow again. Now we could see the woman as she really was, smartly dressed in a black satin evening gown that bared her full white shoulders. She was entering the bedroom, a man in evening clothes at her elbow. The man seemed very nervous, giving occasional glances over his shoulder.

27

"Are you sure we're all alone, Madame Bussy?"

Danielle, fully grown into a glamorous woman, laughed softly. "Certainly, my dear Alphonse. My husband is away on business."

He seemed so nervous, the woman advanced upon him, plucked at his black bow tie, unfastening it. Her hands went to tuxedo jacket, pushing it down his arms. She undid the shirt studs until the stiff-bosomed evening shirt gaped to reveal a hairy chest.

"You finish the rest," she murmured, and went to lift a pack of cigarettes from the night table and strike a match. She breathed in smoke as the man slid out of his trousers, his shirt, until he stood there in his shorts. His body was very excited.

"Now you," he cried.

She laughed at him, making her hips bump, blowing smoke. "Make me want to strip myself for you," she taunted him.

He ran for her, lifted her, dropped with her on the bed. His hands were under the long black satin skirt of the gown, raising it, showing handsome legs in gun-metal nylons to the audience. Up went the skirt, now you could see the full, trembling white thighs and the red lace garters. The man bent and began kissing those soft thighs, up and down.

The woman moaned and lay back. Her legs were lifted, spread wide, the better to permit those worshipping lips to caress her flesh. Occasionally her hips bucked savagely, up and down. When the man settled his mouth into her most intimate parts, she screamed wildly.

Her hands caught his head and held it.

The audience was breathing heavily now as men and women turned to one another, hands lifting skirts and opening trousers. I could hear a woman crying softly, begging her partner to do that to her. I heard knees thump on the cafe floor.

I was not idle myself. My hands had gone under the shaven armpits of the baroness, closing over her heavy breasts. I squeezed them, loosened my grip and then squeezed them again until I had established a rhythm to

28

coincide with the movements of the head buried between those naked white thighs on the stage.

Zia was groaning, letting her hips dance.

The evening gown was on the floor now, the woman on the bed was naked except for her nylons and a red lace garterbelt. The man was thrusting himself between her legs. Her arms, white and lovely with diamond bracelets on them, were clasping him, bringing him to her. Their bodies joined, a cry forcing itself from her lips, a bellow from his. His lips went wild with her stockinged calves protruding on either side of his hips.

I lifted Zia, I ran my hands up under her skirt, discovering that she was wearing only the patterned stockings, held taut by wide frilly garters. Above them and below the micro-skirt, her body was stark naked. My hands went lightly up and down her thighs.

I put pressure on one leg, to get her to lift it. She shook her head, saying swiftly, "*Non, non!* We must not waste your *espadon.*"

"Honey, you don't know me. I'll be this way practically forever. It won't go down."

Her head jerked as she looked into my eyes. Her voice was sharp as she asked, "What's this you're telling me? It won't go down? Pah!"

"It's true. You see, I happen to be afflicted with priapism. As any doctor will tell you, I can keep a perpetual glow on for an indefinite period of time. No woman can exhaust me. It's a medical thing."

In the red glow from the stage, on which the man and woman were still pumping away at one another, Zia's face looked diabolical in its lust. Her tonguetip emerged to lick about her swollen lips as she stared down at my bulging lap.

"I don't believe it. *Chichel* Prove it!"

"What do you think I'm trying to do?"

My hand went to my zipper, but she caught my fingers. Her head shook back and forth. "I don't believe you. Besides, I'm so excited I don't dare take the chance. If you failed me, I'd kill you!"

She freed herself from my hands, slid back into her

29

chair. I sighed. I would have to suffer for a time. The thought touched me that she might be right, that it would be better to wait, that if she too were excited when we got to her bedroom, she might blurt out what I wanted to know about the mermen quickly in order for me to indulge her needs.

I settled back to enjoy the stage show.

The man and woman were shuddering into the orgasmic climax of their act, writhing, using that play of hips and thighs called *culetage* by the French.

As I sat beside Zia von Osterreich, I realized as a secret agent, my priapism was like a secret weapon with which to smite the women with whom I must come in contact. I would make Zia beg for my attentions, compel her to tell me more about the mermen, then give way to our desires.

The performance overhead went into its third stage. The man seated on the straight-backed chair was a different one than he who had performed on the bed. He was a Frenchman with perhaps a trace of Moorish blood in his veins, his skin tones were so swarthy. He held a nude Danielle on his lap, facing away from the audience as her pallid hips went up and down and around in a paroxysm of pleasure.

The sepulchral voice had asked its question, and had been answered with shouts of negation and a thunderous applause. Now we were seeing Danielle at a later time in her life, with her young chauffeur.

I began to suspect Danielle Bussy of being a nymphomaniac.

Frankly I was a little bored. As the Founder of L.S.D., I see enough of this sort of thing without going to a cave cafe for it, but the baroness was enjoying it. She was shifting in her chair, drinking steadily, moving her thighs together. Under the mist of shirtwaist her breasts were swollen hard, with rigid red nipples.

Eyes glazed, mouth a little open, she watched as the woman on stage lifted a thigh and gently, so as not to disengage her attachment to her fellow performer, turned like a chicken on a spit, until her breasts and golden *verger*

30

faced the audience. She picked up the swing and sway of her *cutelage* without missing a beat.

Then we could see the expression on her face: eyes squeezed shut, nostrils vibrating, mouth a little open. Twice she bent her head and her hips pumped madly before an orgasmic shiver rocked her body. Twice she recovered her cool, twice more she let her loins grow amorous.

I began wondering about the young Frenchman. Was he a priapist like myself? I was just about to welcome him mentally to the brotherhood when he gave an ululating scream, his hands fastened like claws in the smooth shoulders of the woman who rode him in the *Venus aversa* position, and he appeared almost to shudder out his life on stage.

The woman leaned forward and fell to the stage floor so everyone could see what was happening to her pleasure partner. Zia moaned and her tongue came out to flick around her lips. There was a faint film of perspiration about her temples where the strands of rich brown hair were plastered.

"I cannot stand much more," she moaned.

I inched my chair closer. "Silly goose, why didn't you say so? I'll give you one of the L.S.D. special treatments in situations like this—when your maidenly modesty refuses to join in the festivities."

Her molten eyes swung sideways. There was a quiver to her lips that smiled faintly. "I forgot you are the *passione*, the expert in sex."

I let my fingertips brush across her left nipple. It did not bend, it was too hard, but her hips shot forward so suddenly she slid to the edge of her chair. Her mouth came open and her eyes squeezed shut. She was breathing harshly and her breasts seemed to dance to that breathing. My fingertips danced across her right nipple.

Zia von Osterreich moaned and shook her head.

"Look around you," I advised. "See for yourself what our fellow drinkers are doing. They don't have any inhibitions."

31

Her eyes slid to a man who held a woman, fully clothed in a black taffeta evening gown, across his lap in imitation of the stage happening. The woman moved her hips like a hula dancer. To their right a woman had her head buried on the lap of her more youthful companion, while his hands clasped her neatly coiffured hair with tugging fingers.

"I could never do that," she murmured. "Not in public."

"Then, in private?"

Her tongue moved wetly around her lips. "*Ja*. In private!"

"Good. Let's go."

I lifted out a few hundred-franc notes from my wallet and dropped them on the table. I hooked her elbow with a hand and lifted her out of the chair. The stage curtain had closed; the audience had been given a breathing space. I was tired of the role of observer, and I wanted in on the action.

I brushed her thigh as she slid past me, heard her gasp as she felt the hard evidence of my own arousal. As she turned away, her hand brushed me as if to make certain of what her thigh had found.

"Don't waste it," she murmured, moving between the tables.

"No fear of that. I've already told you it won't go down. Just relax, believe me—and prepare yourself for nirvana."

She sniffed, but she walked a little faster. I followed her swaying haunches out of the cave casino and up the stone steps to the clear Mediterranean night. A moment before she would have stepped out of the shadows, I reached out, swung her around and drew her in against me.

Her breasts were rocks, her belly a soft pillow. The mouth that yawned to accept my tongue was moist as her neck muscles while she drove her own tongue at mine. She clung to me with all her strength, hips moving steadily.

My fingers worked her mini-skirt up to her hips. Below it she wore only stockings and garter belt and her high-heeled shoes. I bent, I caught her underthighs, I lifted her. I drove forward, hearing her soft cry as she felt the fury of my need, all through her flesh.

"No! Oh, God no! I don't want it like this!"

32

"An hors d'oeuvre only, sweets."

I carried her from the shadows and through the moonlight like that. Her arms were locked about my throat, while her legs, dangling at first as she fought the delight surging through her body, lifted and wrapped themselves about me. She tore her mouth from mine, she let her head fall back as if her neck were broken. She rode ecstasy across the cobblestoned street until the cool metal of the Alfa Romeo door made contact with her bare white buttockflesh.

I had to use force to disengage her arms and legs, to thrust her away so that she leaned panting against the car, staring up at me with wild eyes.

"What kind of man are you to deny me when you practically raped me there outside the door? Are you trying to drive me crazy?"

She was panting and sobbing. Her eyes were big and round. I leaned to kiss the tip of her nose. "Be patient, honey. The night has just begun. You are going to sample a satyr this night. Say I'm punishing you for not having any faith in me."

I opened the door, I shoved her in where she rocked back and forth, hands gripping her nyloned knees. "Devil, devil, devil," she whimpered.

"Exactly. I am Beelzebub, prince of devils. Think pitchforks."

I got in beside her, started the car, and eased it away from the curb. There was a dry wind blowing, brother to the mistral that sweeps across the beaches and the high hills of the Riviera during the winter season. I took the road to Ramatuelle at sixty miles an hour, raising a cloud of dust. Ramatuelle lies close to the pointed rocks at Cap Camarat within viewing distance of the sea.

It is glorious country on the French Riviera. The moon is a silver ball that looks down and chuckles at the men and women who crowd its beaches during the daytime and its shadows when the sun sets, who obey the injunction to love one another with all their hearts. The air is warm, perfumed. It is a land for lovers.

I slid an arm about Zia and drew her over against me.

33

She fought at first, but she let her body go soft when she saw that I had not hidden my manly strength. She gave a soft gasp.

"Did you tell the truth about . . . that?" she asked in a little-girl voice, as if she needed reassurance.

"Absolutely. Word of honor. It's a kind of sickness."

"Sickness!" she breathed.

She was staring, scarcely breathing. Both her hands were shaking. To encourage her, I said, "Go ahead. Make me out a liar, if you can."

A giggle was my answer. "Oh, no. I am taking no chances. I know you men, you are braggarts, most of you." As as afterthought, she murmured, "Liars too."

"Let's bet," I said casually.

"What do you want to bet?" she asked dreamily.

"If I can make you yell 'uncle', if I can tire you out with making love, then you'll tell me what you know about the mermen."

Her head jerked up, her brown eyes staring hard at me. "Why are you so interested in the mermen?"

"They tried to kill you—and me. Why shouldn't I be interested?"

"You sound like a *flic*—a policeman. Are you?"

"No, ma'am. All I want are the facts, ma'am." She was silent, scarcely breathing. I added, "Suppose—just suppose, now—I could do something about the mermen, so they'd never bother you again. How about that?"

"You couldn't."

I am trained to read the inflection of voice tones. It becomes important when you want to make sure a woman means yes when she says no. There was a tiny stab of hope in the baroness' voice when she spoke.

"Maybe not. Maybe yes. What've you got to lose?"

She thought about that silently, then said, "It is true, what you say. The mermen are trying to kill me. What worse thing could they do? And it is a bet you cannot win."

"I can win it all right. My only worry is, will you welch on your bet?"

I had to explain the term to her. When I was done, she

34

shook her head. "No, I will not—what you call—welch on my bet. If I make it."

I did not push. I let her lie with her head on my shoulder and stare down at my manhood. I could feel her hips shift on the car seat, and I caught the muffled breathing she fought to stifle. Once she reached out, gripped me, tightened her fingers.

"All right," she whimpered. "I bet, I bet."

The car was rounding a bend onto the little driveway of her house. I touched the brake, slowing the Alfa Romeo, then swept her up in my arms. I drove my mouth on hers, my hands at her mini-skirt. I hiked it up until she was all bare flesh between the skirt and her stockingtops.

I slid sideways from behind the wheel.

My hands lifted her hips, poised her body, then let it slide downward. She groaned as she knew my full strength. Her head went back and forth as her hips picked up the beat.

"Damn you, damn you! I wanted it indoors, in a bed."

"Don't you like this?" I wondered.

"Of—of co-course I do, but——"

"Then relax and enjoy it."

Her brain did not believe me, but her body did. It leaped and flopped; it drove and darted. Her breath was a gale of perfume against my cheeks as she brought her lips to my face, as she began kissing all over my nose and eyes and chin, blinding me when I sought to open the glove compartment of the car.

"Darling, oh, darling! Never stop! Never stop!"

I opened the door. I caught her underthighs in my hands, I raised her, slid my feet out. We made it, with my feet on the ground and her legs locked around my hips. My hand fumbled in the glove compartment, drew out the flat packet I call my sex survival kit. Zia paused in her kissing long enough to ask me if this wasn't tiring on me.

"Not yet. Besides, you're the one who's going to be tired before the night ends, remember?"

Her laughter was an echo out of Sodom and Gomorrah as I carried her like that away from the car and toward her

35

houe. She spasmed and went limp three times before I got her key into the lock and turned it. She was really hung up on me.

I let her go her own way once the door was open. Her hand switched on a light. Then she sagged against the door jamb, shaking her head and staring at me, panting to get her breath back.

"You're unbelievable," she whispered.

"I hate to say it but I told you so."

Her arm came up about my neck. She kissed me hungrily, then whispered, "But I'm not nearly done. Not nearly!"

"I should hope not," I chuckled. "To paraphrase a saying, I have not yet begun to f—" Her soft palm covered my mouth.

"Don't talk. Just follow me," she murmured.

I ran behind her shapely stockinged legs, bare thighs and buttocks, up a narrow stair to the second floor. A lamp jumped to life. I found myself in something out of a New England ski lodge, all flowered chintz, maple and walnut, with a couple of hooked rugs on the floor. It was a feminine room, with a touch of jasmine in the air, a memory of warm bathwater and soapsuds, of perfume atomizers and dainty underthings.

I am a sybarite at heart. To me, a woman is fragrance and flesh, delicacy and hidden lusts. She is beauty and a kind of happy wickedness, a flower in bloom and a claw in a velvet glove. The Delphic oracle, the Mater Magna and Messalina, all wrapped up in skin like a rose petal.

Zia put a hand to the buttons of her blouse.

Her smile was a temptation and a challenge. She did not have to speak; I could read the message in her eyes. She was daring me to exhaust her, in more ways than one.

CHAPTER THREE

The blouse hung loose, and I could see the inner slopings of her big white breasts, startlingly white against the chocolate tan of her shoulders and midriff. As she moved, her breasts swung back and forth lazily and her rigid brown nipples scratched the misty nylon of the shirtwaist.

Her smile was deliciously lewd.

Her tanned shoulders went back, the blouse slipped to her upper arms and downward. Her breasts fell out into the lamplight, shaking. I stepped forward, caught them in my hands, bent to kiss them. She breathed faster.

"Your garters," I murmured.

"What?" she asked dazedly.

I knelt before her. On each thigh she had put a Gay Nineties garter, all red and black lace. I slipped them off as she looked down in complete curiosity. I got up and doubled the garters over.

I slipped the garters over her breasts so that they were compressed and made more tumescent by their constraint. I stepped back and smiled.

Her eyes lifted from her gartered breasts to me. "You have a thing about breasts?"

"It's to add to the pleasure, your highness."

Her slim brown eyebrows drew together. "I don't understand."

"You will. You see, the squeezing process of the garters will make your *lolos* much more sensitive. Give it a little time."

"Is this something you teach in your League for Sexual Dynamics?" she mocked, half laughing.

37

"Don't knock it until you've tried it."

She shimmied her shoulders and gasped. "Oh," she said. "Oh!"

I began to take my own clothes off, while she went on shimmying, staring with wide eyes as more and more of my body came into view. When I plucked off the last sock and stood naked, she gave a little cry and caught her breasts in her hands.

Her eyes flamed as her fingers squeezed. "*Ja, ja!* It is what you say! It is—more exciting this way!"

When the breasts are erotically aroused, their blood vessels fill up, the breasts swell, the nipples enlarge, I explained. The garters would then act like valves to keep the blood in the mammary veins, so that the breasts cannot deflate but remain in that sensually exciting tumescence until the garters are removed.

She asked, "Now what?"

I bent and lifted my sex survival kit, undoing the snaps, throwing back the flat black lid. The baroness came two steps closer, her stockinged legs like passion pillars alongside me.

"What's that?"

"The L.S.D. kit for sex survival."

I fitted three sulphur rings on the middle finger of my right hand. They were much, much too large, so I took them off.

"What are they for?"

"Silly girl! Come find out."

I paused to unzip her crumpled skirt, helped her slide her bare buttocks—they looked very pale beside the tan of her belly and thighs—out of the mini-skirt. I lifted two large pillows, fluffed them, then dropped them on the edge of the bed.

She sat down on the pillows, eyes wide as I slipped on the sulphur rings. From time immemorial, man has sought to make Nature even better. Sulphur rings are brothers to the silver clasp employed by Hsi-men Ch'ing as related in the Chin P'ing Mei. These pleasure rings clasp the male member, helping it to prolong erection while at the same

38

time stimulating the vaginal walls of the female. The sulphur in the ring I was going to employ works as an astringent to tighten the vaginal walls so as to add to the pleasure of the baroness.

I moved into position between her thighs. "We shall begin with the ostrich tail position of the Arab erotologists—the *hachou en nekanok*."

"Begin with?" she asked, falling on her back, which was necessarily lower than her hips because of the pillows beneath her behind.

"To be sure, begin with. In all, there are thirty-six positions that we shall sample. So begin slowly, and swiftly, as the runner says."

"Mon Dieu! Trente-six!"

I gripped the undersides of her knees, pushed them back and upwards so that her tanned legs, upright above her head, formed the tail of an ostrich while only her head and shoulders remained on the bed. I drove deep. Zia convulsed, mouth and eyes wide open. To the ancient Arabs, the love art was devotedly studied as any astronomer might study the stars. Each movement, each change in posture, was duly and aptly named.

In my role as sexologist, I believe that the study of human relationships between the sexes in the love act is the most single important phase of our existence. Most people do not know the name of a star, or how to find the angle of declination; few people have to fix a carburetor, or apply the value of pi; but everybody experiences sex during his or her lifetime. And the more skillful one is at it, the better it is for himself and his partner.

Unfortunately our western world lags behind the east in this. Our Eastern brothers—Arabs, Indians, Persians—understand and value the love relationships. They have made a learning out of what, to Americans or English, Germans or Italians or Swedes, should come naturally. This is not so. There is an ability to excel at sex given to all of us, if we properly understand and apply its rules and methods of application.

I continued with the ostrich tail posture, pointing out to

39

the baroness—as if she couldn't feel it—that the resultant depth of penetration was increased almost two fold by the backward thrust of her legs, which forced her genital region forward. The sulphur rings were merely an added excitant, but such a powerful one, due both to their size, clamped about my continually moving member, and to their astringent qualities, that Zia must have existed only at one point in her body. She cried out her delight, mouth wide open and wailing, as her head began a metronomic rhythm on the bed. Her body trembled in reaction to the strain of her position, but this appeared only to heighten the intensity of her ecstasy.

The French tickler, the ampalang and other devices with lengths of hair or bits of feathers added, are mere variations on the sulphur rings, which prevent the male member from becoming overly excited. Thus the male orgasm is delayed. But I used the rings, not for my own sake, but for that of the baroness.

Zia dug the sulphur rings. Did she ever!

Her hips were gyrating, looping, lifting and driving. By this time, unconsciously forming the *el mordefeda*—the manner of the frog—she had fastened the heels of her Pappagallos on the edge of the bed for greater leverage so that the powerful muscles of her thighs could control and regulate the angle of penetration and the level of depth. The scraping of the sulphur rings along the vaginal walls—though, strictly speaking, there are few nerve endings in the vaginal channel itself—were an added excitation that drove screams of wild delight from her corded throat.

I angled my own thrusts to involve her distended clitoral bud in the goings-on. The female epicenter of erotism is located in the clitoris and in the *labia minora*. Any application of the male thrust to include these regions builds a pleasure so intense as almost to become unbearable.

We swung into the *el mokefa* posture, which is a variation on the others, in which the female places her underthighs against my chest so that her calves cross about my neck, without missing a beat. I drove forward as the Shayk Nefzawi advises, firmly and with the necessary hip movements, to vary the piston pulse beat.

The baroness keened her appreciation in a thick cry.

"Now for the *el khouraki,* your highness."

"No, please! Let me rest!"

"Already? We're only on posture four!"

"But I can't take any m-m-more!"

I laughed. "You don't know your own strength, honey. Give it all you've got and I'll introduce you to the new Baroness von Osterreich."

Her gartered breasts were swollen beyond belief, they looked like turgid white balloons, tipped with intensely large brown nipples. I bent double and licked those nipples with my tongue. Her sensation was intensified by the strangulating garters. She screamed and screamed, hips lurching out of control.

I moved her leg and swung her body around.

"The fourth posture, your highness. The *vyompada-uttana* of the Hindus. On your side—ah, that's it. We aren't taking them in textbook order, you understand. I don't want things to get dull for you!"

"Oh, my God," she breathed, shifting and lifting a leg.

I assumed the proper *a'sana* and drove deep. Zia shuddered. Her hips moved gently. The side posture is for gentleness, for prolonged enjoyment. On my side, with my leg uplifted above her hip and resting on it, I was able to move in a steady rhythm without tiring my muscles. This is the difference between the eastern and the western philosophy of making love. The easterner goes about it slowly, he sips tea, he nibbles upon fruit or nuts, he even smokes a pipe sometimes. The idea is to make it last. No easterner worthy of the name is a slam-bang-thank-you-ma'am lover.

Neither is Rod Damon. I stroked, I showered thrills on her erogenous zones, I drove her off into that state of bliss the Japanese name *gokuraku-ojo.* There was a dreaming little smile on her full lips. Her breasts shook only very slightly, due to the tightened garters, but the flesh of her pallid hips and tanned thighs jellied and shimmied to my poundings.

Her arms went around me, holding me close. She was

41

peaking again, and then again, head flung back, her lips losing their contented smile and twisting in a grotesquerie of pleasure that made it seem as if she were in pain.

I let her savor ecstasy for long moments before I moved her again. "Sit up, my love. We are switching to the *upavishta* postures."

"No. Please, no. Just let me lie here," she protested.

I sat cross-legged in the yogi pose. I caught her wrist and drew her across the rumpled bedcovers. "You sit—so. Upon me. Lock your legs behind my back in the proper *padm-asana*. Do you understand?"

She was balanced on one knee and a foot on the bed. Her hair spilled down about her shoulders and there were the beginnings of dark rings under her eyes. From my upstanding manhood her eyes glanced at a wall clock.

"It's almost dawn," she pointed out.

"Night, day, what's the difference?"

"You aren't real," she murmured.

"I'm real enough. Now you see what I meant back at the Diabolique. I just don't go down. Come on, come on. I'm still ready for love."

Zia made a face, rubbing her privacy. "I ache," she admitted. "Can't we postpone this for a little while? I need a bath, a shower."

"Do I win my bet?"

Her eyes turned gleeful. "Tell you what. If you can take a little torture yourself, I'll say 'uncle'."

"What've you got in mind?"

The baroness lay down on the coverlets and let her hands slide between my crossed legs. Her fingertips were soft as they caressed my manhood. She inched forward, mouth a little open.

"The gift of love Cleopatra gave to Caesar?"

"Mmmmm—something like that."

"Wait, then. Let me really enjoy it."

Her face looked stunned, then angry. She sat up, her breasts scarcely moving in their black and red lace garters. "If you're trying to insult me, Professor Damon, I don't——"

42

"Don't be so snesitive. All I want is my sexual survival kit."

Zia hesitated, then laughed, shaking her head. She got off the bed and padded in her nyloned feet—she had kicked off her Pappagallos long ago, and her expensive nylons were tattered, with a dozen runs in each leg—across the room to the bureau where my kit lay. She turned a curious gaze on me.

"Now what?"

"You'll find a tiny vial inside. Oil of wintergreen."

She drew out the vial, held it up. "This?"

"Put a drop of that in a glass of water and gargle."

Thin brown eyebrows arched. "Before I—?"

"Of course, before. This is for my pleasure."

She shrugged, and went into the bathroom. I heard water running. In a little while I heard the sound of gargling. Then she was coming back toward me, smiling faintly.

"Honestly, you're the most amazing man I've ever met. What does the wintergreen do?"

"Sorry, but I can't demonstrate that. It's a man-thing."

She pushed me flat. "None of this yogi stuff when I perform. I'm a simple creature." Her palm closed on me and squeezed. Then she was sliding down at right angles to my body, resting her cheek on my belly and removing the sulphur rings one after the other.

Her hand caressed at first. Then she drew me toward her lips, kissing gently. Her tongue came out. When I moaned, Zia giggled.

Moist lips closed upon me. I shuddered. The oil of wintergreen gargle adds a new dimension to this oldest of all love kisses. It bites the flesh; it invigorates it; it stings and soothes; it burns; it becalms. In moments, my entire body was shuddering as if I were having a fit.

Zia went on and on. Her head bobbed, then rested so that her lips and tongue and teeth could take over. She moaned in a kind of masochistic madness. Your true fellatrix has something of the masochist in her. She has the desire to be submissive before the male and demonstrates this side of her psyche by offering to please him without being pleased herself.

43

Her role then becomes a minor one between the two sexes. She is giving of herself without taking. She shows herself to be not quite the equal of the male master. Whether this applied to the baroness, I did not know; there are many reasons for the act. Every human being ever born has an impulse toward oral eroticism. The impulse may be strong or weak, according to the individual.

She drew her lips away after half an hour, and lay limp. Very faintly I heard her whisper, "Uncle, uncle. I'm beat. I can't move another muscle. So—uncle! Goddamnit! There! Uncle! Uncle! Uncle!"

I patted her hip.

"You were beautiful, baby. Beautiful. Everything I'd hoped you'd be. Now just be something a little more. Start telling me about those mermen."

She shivered and rose to a sitting position.

"Mind if I put something on? It's a long story, and it's chilly now that we aren't making love."

She slipped into a chenille robe after stripping off her ruined stockings. Then she plumped out the pillows, putting them near the headboard of her queen-size bed. She lay down with her head on my shoulder, my arm about her, and began to talk.

"About a year ago I met Ernst Bachmann."

Ernst Bachmann was an East German scientist, a specialist in biochemistry. He was on vacation in Athens. He met the baroness over a cup of *cafe Tourkiko* at the Grande Bretagne hotel. They felt an instant admiration for each other.

He was a handsome man, tall and physically strong, with a Germanic arrogance that appealed to her feminine instincts in some perverse manner she could not understand. He wined and dined her at Floca's and at the Papparika; he went swimming with her at Verkiza beach; he danced with her to romantic music at the Galaxy, on the Hilton roof.

He also made love to her. To his precise scientific mind, love-making was merely a matter of indulging the human body, to rid itself of accumulated tensions. Zia von Oster-

44

reich taught him that sex could be fun. For two weeks he became a youth again, with her. He was rich, with a family fortune behind him. He had never had a wife nor a mistress, and he begged her to become his mistress.

Zia had been at odds and ends with herself, so she agreed. She traveled to Majorca with him, to Rome, finally to the Greek island of Thraxos in the Aegean Sea. Ernst Bachmann had a laboratory compound on Thraxos.

At first she thought he was engaged in studying marine biology. His laboratory was filled with huge glass tanks in which swam all types and manner of fish. There were herring and whiting, tunny and sardines, mussels and oysters and crawfish, and, of course, the dolphin. There were even Portuguese men-o'-war and sea horses. Bachmann spent almost all of his time on Thraxos with his tanks and appeared to be most dedicated to his calling.

One night, quite by accident, Zia lost her way in the mazelike compound, and found herself in a room which she had never seen before. There was a large glass tank—and there was a man sleeping in it. The tank was not empty, it was filled with water. The man was breathing the water as does a fish.

She stood rooted to the spot, not quite believing what she saw. She tiptoed closer. By the faint blue light that illumined the room, she could make out the man's chest, faintly lifting, faintly falling. There was no doubt about it. The man was able to live in water.

Suddenly terrified—she was intelligent enough to understand the political possibilities behind such a discovery—Zia ran from the chamber. Her thoughts were chaotic. She wanted out of this predicament at once. Ernst Bachmann would not hear of it. He enjoyed her sensual skills too much to be rid of her.

The baroness realized she was a prisoner. From being his mistress, she had turned into his sex slave. Though she enjoyed the sex, she knew damn well Bachmann would grow tired of her in time and might then kill her to keep her quiet about his laboratory location.

She had nothing but her body to use as a bribe. Fortunately a strong young fisherman became enamored of her. Her flesh was better than gold, in his judgment, so one stormy night he took her to the mainland in his dinghy. She spent a week with him, then cabled her bankers in Geneva for funds. She flew to Rome, and lost herself for a while among the masses. Only lately had she dared come out into the open.

Head nestled against my shoulder, she spread her hands. With a rueful smile, she murmured, "You see what it has brought me? A near miss with death."

"And me," I added.

She turned her head to kiss my jaw. "Darling! Of course, you."

I grinned, "I'm not just a good roll in the hay, love. Might be I could get Bachmann off your back."

She wriggled around so she could look into my eyes. "So? You are not just the playboy professor on a vacation, *Hein?* You are something else. But what?"

"Let's just say I have a hobby. I'd like you to meet a friend of mine. No names are necessary. I call him Walrus-moustache. So can you."

"Where is this Walrus-moustache?"

"Somewhere over the Atlantic, at a guess. He's flying here from the States. I know he'll want to meet you. How about it?"

She was thoughtful, lower lip projecting. At last she shrugged. "Why not? I have nothing to lose but my life. And I'm going to lose that anyhow, unless somebody does something about Ernst."

I slid down under the covers, drawing her with me.

"Sleep now. Say later."

I kissed her pouting lips.

The Riviera sunlight woke me by shining through the Venetian blinds into my eyes. I rolled over to shut it out, but a hand came down flat on my exposed flank, driving away the sleepiness.

"Up, lazybones!" Zia shouted gaily. "To the rescue, my brave knight."

"Yeah, hey," I mumbled.

46

I let her drag me out of bed and push me under a cold shower. I woke up good then. I put the warm water on, grabbed a bar of soap, and spent a quarter of an hour at my ablutions. I also shaved.

I ate my *petit déjeuner* in a sunny breakfast nook with Zia across the table from me in something pink and frilly by Dior. We feasted on curried eggs and sausages, with hot coffee and freshly baked muffins. It was almost like being married.

"Give me an hour," she promised when we were done.

I phoned the hotel. Walrus-moustache had not arrived.

But as I was braking in front of the Hotel de la Tour, a big black touring car swung into the curb ahead of me. I needed no second look to recognize one of its two passengers as Walrus-moustache. He got out, turned, bowed to me, raked the baroness with his wise eyes, then proceeded on into the hotel lobby, his friend at his elbow.

The friend was introduced to us later as Norman Beltinge, a marine biologist from an eastern university in the United States. He was a lean man, rather tall, with a sprinkling of gray in his pale blonde hair. His blue eyes were calm and emotionless behind black-rimmed glasses.

In the privacy of my room, Zia told her story. As she spoke, Walrus-moustache kept glancing at Beltinge. When Beltinge did not sound off about science fiction hogwash, but seemed very impressed, the chief relaxed.

When the baroness was done, Walrus-moustache asked, "How about it, Norm? Could what her highness says be possible?"

"Oh, yes. Very much so. We've made enormous strides in physiology within the past five years. Men have demonstrated that small mammals like a hamster or a mouse can live in water. That is, they can extract the oxygen they need for life from the water itself."

Walrus-moustache frowned. "How's that again?"

Inside a membranous cage, a hamster had been lowered into a tank filled with water and fish. The hamster had been able to extract its needed oxygen from the water, since the membranous walls of its little cage had filtered out every-

47

thing from the water but the oxygen. Though the silicone-rubber membrane had no holes in it, it was porous enough to permit oxygen molecules to seep through into the chamber where the hamster could breathe them.

"It's a form of osmosis," Beltinge went on, "which has been common knowledge for some years. But only when the principle was applied to the silicone membrane was a demonstrable technique invented for its marine use."

The membrane could also be used in space travel, Beltinge pointed out, the better to assist in draining off the water vapor of an astronaut's perspiration. Walrus-moustache waved an impatient hand.

"Never mind that. Get back to its marine uses," he muttered.

"It's been theorized that a membrane for a man could be constructed too, but it woulld have to be at least sixty square feet in size for him to get the oxygen he needs."

Zia shook her head. "The man I saw had no membrane tank about him."

Beltinge was bursting with eagerness as he turned to her. "No, no, highness! I am certain your Ernst Bachmann has done more than that. I am explaining how our science has advanced, step by step like a baby learning to walk.

"The membrane is only one facet of the research."

There was also a liquid that had been discovered, called fluorocarbon, into which a mouse could be totally submerged and still breathe without any membranous material being used at all. The fluorocarbon was literally overloaded with oxygen, which the mouse was able to breathe, since it holds more than thirty times as much oxygen as air itself.

"It is hoped that this liquid can be used to cure deep-sea divers of the bends, which can kill, as you know, when a man comes up through layers of varying pressures in the ocean too suddenly. It's caused by the compressed nitrogen in the air they breathe from their oxygen tanks, getting into their bloodstreams. Instead of compressed air, if the deep-sea divers breathe in fluorocarbon liquid, it will prevent those bends."

Soft street noises came in through the windows with the

beams of sunlight. Zia crossed her nyloned legs, the stockings made a slithering sound for a moment. Walrus-moustache shifted in his chair and scowled.

"All very well—but how can Bachmann accomplish what he's supposed to have done?"

Beltinge said, "I can only theorize. From what her highness tells me, I shall assume that Bachmann has developed an injectant which when placed inside a human body—perhaps after an operation or two—will permit him to breathe in sea water, extract the needed oxygen from it, then reject everything but the oxygen. Perhaps by silicone membrane gills placed in the throat. I can't narrow it down much closer than that."

The chief nodded, "It's good enough. We know what's been done, to some extent. Damon fought two men who could breathe under water. He killed them both, but he didn't drown them. That's important. They didn't need diving equipment, scuba gear or oxygen tanks to go about their dirty business.

"I accept the fact. Now I want to know—how come?"

He squirmed about until he was facing me. "Doctor, you're going to that Greek island, just as soon as I can arrange transportation. You're going to swipe Bachmann's notes or notebooks. I want his researches for our own scientists to work on."

His heavy fist slammed the chair arm. "Damnation! Do you realize what we may have uncovered?"

He paused a moment, heavily tufted eyebrows meeting above his nose. "Do any of you remember what happened in December of 1967? Eh? In Australia?"

I cleared my throat. "Are you talking about the drowning of former Prime Minister Harold Holt? How he was killed by sharks while swimming off Cheviot Beach?"

"I am. But how do you know sharks killed him? His body was never found, though the resources of an entire nation were utilized to find it. Now suppose—I'm just talking, you understand, I'm not accusing anybody—suppose a couple of these mermen lay in wait for him? Eh? Holt was a good friend to the United States. Maybe somebody wanted to get rid of him. Russia? Red China? North Viet Nam? Who knows?"

His face was furrowed in thought. He slapped the chair arm again. "I'm thinking about underwater armies too. Soldiers with weapons ejected from the hatch of half a hundred submarines who can swim underwater to shore, do some mighty important damage, then swim out of sight back to their submarines. No scuba equipment to slow them down, just their weapons and whatever else they need to do their job. Eh? How does that hit you?"

"Below the belt," I murmured.

He nodded. "It damn well does. Another thing! In January of sixty-eight, the Israelis lost a submarine under mighty mysterirous circumstances in the eastern Mediterranean. The *Dakar*. It had sixty-nine men aboard it. The same week, the French lost a submarine named the *Minerva*. Same mysterious circumstances. Suppose again that an underwater force of half a dozen mermen attacked each submarine, slapped magnetic mines against its hull—and blew them up.

"Those men wouldn't need equipment either, to bog them down. They could be damn well naked—excuse me, your highness!—except for flippers on their feet and magnetic mines in their hands. No need to surface, no need to let anybody in this whole wide world know they were there. They swim to their target; they do what they've been ordered to do; they disappear—probably back into the submarine that brought them. As far as the world can discover—it was only some freak accident that destroyed the *Dakar* and the *Minerva*."

The hairs were standing up on the back of my neck. I was imagining mermen climbing out of the sea on the beaches of the world, spraying people with machine-gun fire, and then disappearing back into the briny deep. Talk about your terrorists! Or maybe some higher echelon figure in a world government might be fishing, or taking a boat ride. Merman appears. Merman tosses hand grenade. Whoooosh! No more important government figure. The merman would leave no clues behind him, nobody could

50

even hazard a guess at his identity. The government which had despatched him to kill would be able to turn an innocent face to the world.

I shivered. Zia was trying to scratch a match to light a cigarette and was failing because her hands were shaking so much. Norman Beltinge was biting his lower lip, looking worried.

"About that transportation," I said.

Zia got her cigarette going and waved a hand. "I may be able to help there. Some friends of mine are vacationing in the Mediterranean. Their yacht, a big one that cost two million dollars in England to build, is in port right now. The *Athena*, it's called."

I remembered seeing it anchored just outside the harbor.

"Will they accept me as a guest?" I wondered.

Zia smiled, "You'd be better off to hire on as a steward. A steward goes everywhere, sees just about everything. You could go places you might not be admitted as a fellow guest."

Chalk one up for the baroness.

"Okay, then—as a steward. But what I don't know about being a steward would fill a five-foot bookshelf."

Zia laughed delightedly. "Silly! A steward does almost anything. You can have a dining room steward, cabin steward, bath steward, and a deck steward. On a private yacht like the *Athena*, you'd probably be all those things rolled into one."

"Sounds great. Like maybe working in a salt mine."

The baroness giggled. "Oh, it isn't all that bad. You probably won't have to wait on table—they have somebody for that job. Your main problem would be personal services—furnishing dramamine tablets for seasick people, maybe getting a suit pressed or a dress dry-cleaned, bring deck chairs when they're needed, or getting a book for an insomniac to while away the sleepless hours."

"Boy of all trades," I agreed.

Walrus-moustache asked, "Do your friends need a steward?"

"Not that I know of. I just happen to have heard that

51

Emile, their present steward, is homesick. The Fortescus, who own the yacht, are always on the go. Emile hasn't been home to Paris, where his wife and children live, for over a year. I have the feeling that if somebody offered him a few thousand francs, he'd jump ship with a yell of pure delight."

Walrus-moustache nodded. "Good. I'll contribute the francs. Can you arrange for some sort of meeting between the professor and this Emile?"

"This morning, if you'd like. Emile is always to be found on the Quai Jean Jaures for a bowl of soup at one of its restaurants as a kind of brunch, a combination of breakfast and lunch."

Zia let her eyes dance up at me. "You will have to let me conduct the talk, *mon ami*. No matter what I say to Emile, you must agree. If you do, you will be a steward on the *Athena* by nightfall."

"He'll agree," growled the chief.

Zia stood up. "Shall we go, then? It's a little past eleven. If we dawdle, Emile may be gone. And from the gossip around town, the *Athena* will hoist anchor sometime tomorrow."

"So soon?" I muttered, thinking about leaving the baroness and not liking it. She read my thoughts and patted my cheek.

"You shall be my knight errant, darling. And when you return, I shall be here to give you your reward. I promise that."

Walrus-moustache grunted, heaving himself to his feet. He does not hold with romantic nonsense. To him it was enough that I was going to save the world for democracy (what, again?). He fished in his pocket and brought out a roll of bills that his hand could not contain.

"It's French currency," he told me, thrusting it in my palm. "Use as much of it as you need. I'll be waiting in my own rooms for a report. Damn, but I'm tired. This time differential between the States and Europe always bothers me."

He went clumping off with Norman Beltinge at his elbow. We listened to their footfalls until they died out. Then I turned to Zia.

"I didn't realize you wanted to get rid of me so fast," I more or less snarled. "I thought you'd had yourself a ball last night."

She threw her soft feminine attributes against me. "Darling, I did! I did! I want to stay with you forever—but if you can save my life? Think, dearest! I will be yours forever. I will be able to devote myself to you completely!"

"Yeah, well—maybe."

She bit my chin. "Besides, wait until you see Ilona Fortescu or Fleur Devot or Celeste Maillot. They will make you forget all about me."

"Not a chance," I vowed, kissing her kissable lips.

"Bet?" she murmured, glancing at me from under her long-lashed eyes. "Darling, I know you better than you know yourself. When the chance comes for a little carnal research with a Greek social registrite or a French starlet, you'll snap at it."

"Greek, huh?"

The baroness shook her head at me reprovingly. "Shame on you, Rod. Your mind is always in the gutter."

"I'm just thinking about my job," I replied loftily.

We went down the stairs and out into the sunlight. The Quai Jean Jaures was only a few hundred yards away. It was good to walk in the sunlight and breathe in the salt air as it swept across the harbor to roam through St. Tropez. Zia paused, caught my arm and pointed out the huge white hulk of the *Athena,* riding at anchor in the Baie des Canoubiers.

"She's a beauty," I nodded.

"For two million dollars, she ought to be."

We went on toward the quai. There, in front of what is called the old town, there are many little shops separated by nothing more elegant than chicken wire fences. The houses lean outward a little, since they are very old. The newer homes are straight up and down. The new houses were built after the Germans blew up the port in 1944 to prevent it from falling into Allied hands when it was attacked. The destruction did them no good, they surrendered that very afternoon from the citadel where they had retired to put up a last-ditch resistance.

Emile Crillon was sitting alone at a round table, rubbing his hands together before tackling his bowl of steaming fish soup. A napkin was tucked into his leathery brown neck, his black eyes were sparkling with anticipated pleasure, and he had covered his bald pate with a seaman's cap.

He scowled at sight of me, but his eyes danced when he saw Zia. He started to get up but she pushed him back down into his seat, telling him to eat.

"Me, I'm thirsty," she said, with a look at me.

I ordered a bottle of Vin Rouge to be served, as was the custom, at room temperature. I gave Emile the biggest glass and kept it filled. It was easy to order more bottles.

"Emile, do me a favor," Zia begged when he pushed the empty bowl away from him.

"Anything, highness."

"Go home to your family. Take a gift of five thousand francs and retire. You ought to be in the Halles market, buying crayfish, boiling them yourself, kissing your Marie and all your children good night."

Emile Crillon gulped. "Five thousand francs? For me?"

Zia gestured. "Give it to him please."

I peeled off the five thousand new francs—which amounted to one thousand American dollars—and then threw in another thousand on my own. Walrus-moustache could afford it. Emile stared at me, at Zia, and at the money. His eyes misted over with tears.

"For the past three years I have wanted to quit. Now you come along like an angel and make it possible. May *le bon Dieu* have you always in His mind." Suddenly his face grew tragic. "Ah, *parbleu!* What am I thinking? I have the steward job on the *Athena!* I could not desert them now."

"Not if I had a replacement, Emile?"

He beamed. "A replacement? Who?"

Zia jerked her thumb at me. Emile turned his leathery neck to study me. "You are a sailor? You have been a steward?"

"Well, not exactly."

54

"He can carry pills. He can lift deck chairs."

Emile cackled laughter. *"Oui, oui.* And he can maybe entertain the ladies better than I can, yes? But it is not to be thought of. My post is too important to——"

Zia leaned closer. *"Mon ami, mon cher ami*—do me the favor? I am tired of his love-making. I want to get rid of him. Now be a good fellow."

More laughter, cackling out of that leathery throat. "Aha! So? Now it comes out. You want the *Athena* to do your burial work, do you? So you can find a new romance? Well, now."

If there is one argument that will always work with a Frenchman, it is a romantic one. His scrawny fingers were clasping the six thousand francs with the tenacity of a bulldog's jaw, but it needed the added spur of romance to compel Emile Crillon to see the light.

He shrugged expansively, as if against his will. "I will do what I can. I swear this on the Virgin. I will go to the yacht with your, ah, friend. I will ask the boss, M'sieu Fortescu. If he says yes, I shall retire."

Zia leaned forward, clasped his head and kissed his windburned cheeks. Emile beamed. Me, I sat there like a scorned lover.

Half an hour later I was sitting in a powerboat beside Emile Crillon, listening to him babble on about his duties aboard the *Athena.* The powerboat was driven by a man in a sea beret, blue and white, a blue and white striped jersey, and blue duck sailor pants. I gathered this was the more or less official uniform of the yacht crew.

We went up a ladder alongside the hundred-and-ninety-foot *Athena.* It was one of the largest private ships in the world. It would sleep a dozen passengers and a crew of twenty. It had a big galley for the passengers, a smaller one for the crew. Its engines could develop almost eighteen-hundred horsepower, and her tanks stored enough fuel for a fourteen-hundred-mile cruise. Those engines permitted the *Athena* to speed at close to sixteen knots per hour.

There was a woman lying on the sun deck in a black bikini when we came off the ladder. We walked forward, and saw that she was asleep. Emile cleared his throat several times until the woman stirred, lifting her attractive face, shading her eyes under a palm.

"Yes, Emile? What is it?"

"I am sorry to trouble you, madame. It is the matter of my retirement. I am quitting ship, but I have brought a replacement."

The woman stirred again, lifting glossy black hair out of her eyes the better to see me. She was still half asleep, but I saw her eyes open a little as she propped herself up on her elbows. Two heavy breasts hung down between her arms, unburdened by any covering. Suddenly she smiled.

"Well! Is this your replacement, Emile?"

"*Oui,* madame."

"What's your name?"

"Damon, ma'am. Rod Damon. I'm an impoverished professor on a sabbatical. I want to do a little research on the Greek islands. I can't afford to go there except by working my way."

She put a forearm across her breasts, hiding the nipples. Her other arm she waved in the air. "My robe, Emile. My robe—*va vite.*"

I was there ahead of him, scooping up the terry cloth robe, holding it so she could place her arms in its sleeves. Over her bare shoulders, her green eyes looked up at me. To slip into the robe meant she must draw her forearm away from her breasts. She understood it; she knew I did too. Her mouth curved into a faint smile.

"A professor, you say?"

"I am the founder of the League for Sexual Dynamics, madame. I am also a sociology professor."

"Sexual dynamics," she murmured thoughtfully. "What does that mean?"

She slid her left arm into the sleeve, but she kept her right forearm up as a shield before her nipples. Over her right shoulder I murmured, "I teach boys and girls the proper attitudes and techniques of sex, madame. I seek to instill into them the understanding that sex is good, clean and wholesome, an important part of life and therefore to be appreciated in various ways and methods."

The forearm dropped. I was treated to a full view of the

56

Fortescu breasts as they wobbled slightly while she tried to find the sleeve with her right hand. My fingers were clamped on the sleeve, which effectively prevented her from getting her arm inside it, making her fumble more, which resulted in making her *lolos* jounce up and down and sideways.

"*Ravissante,*" I murmured.

She turned her head and stared at me. For a moment I wondered if I had gone too far. I did not know Ilona Fortescu. She might feel I had insulted her. If she did, and I did not get the steward job, I might have signed Zia von Osterreich's death warrant.

CHAPTER FOUR

Ilona Fortescu turned away from the boat deck, facing the
empty Mediterranean, so that the only one who could see
her naked breasts was myself. I did not know this wife of
the Greek industrialist, but I felt I knew women. No
woman is completely angry at a man who pays her body
compliments.

I did not look at her face. I kept my eyes fastened on her
large brown nipples, and I let my admiration show. she
smiled faintly and shrugged.

"Are you through admiring me?" she asked softly.

"I could never be through admiring you. You're
beautiful."

"You're a naughty young man."

"Am I naughty—because I admire beauty? What was it
Keats said? A thing of beauty is a joy forever. Yes. You are
a living painting by a master. Da Vinci? Raphael?
Definitely not a Rubens."

Her delighted laughter rang out. "Take your hand away
from my sleeve, you libertine."

"Libertine? Me?" I protested innocently.

I let her slide her arm into the sleeve and draw the robe
about her bosom. Her cheeks were flushed and her eyes
were bright. She was the eternal woman, knowing she has
made a male conquest.

She reached up and tapped my cheek with her fingertips.
"*Oui*, you. A libertine of the worst sort—one who is attractive to, and is attracted by, women. Oh, I know your
kind all right."

"And?" I challenged, smiling.

Emile cleared his throat. Almost irritated, Madame Fortescu threw him a glance. "Yes, Emile? Oh, you want your back pay, I suppose. Well, come along." She glanced over her shoulder at me. "You too, Professor."

In the office where her husband kept his fingers on the pulse of his vast industrial empire, Ilona Fortescu lifted out a sheaf of banknotes from a safe. She counted out his back pay and added a month's wages as a parting bonus for Emile. The leathery little man beamed.

"Will you be able to go to work at once, Professor?" she asked, turning her attention to me.

"Just as soon as I get my few belongings from town."

"Emile, help him," she ordered.

She stood there with her chenille robe folded about her curves as I bowed my way out of the little office and followed Emile Crillon across the deck to the boarding ladder. Her green eyes glowed, and there was a catlike smile on her full mouth.

On the way to shore, Emile told me my uniform would be a blue blazer and white duck trousers, white shirt and dark blue tie. The blazer would have the arms of the house of Fortescu sewn on the handkerchief pocket. I owned a blue blazer, I could buy a few pair of white ducks in town.

Zia was waiting when we landed. I told her everything as she accompanied me to my room where I packed my pigskin luggage. With true female perspicacity, she zeroed in on the facts.

"Ilona Fortescu likes you, doesn't she?"

"Now, now. I just made a good impression."

"I'll bet. And it's all my fault. Will I ever learn?"

"I'm your knight, remember?"

Zia laughed, restored to good humor. "All right. *Touché*! But I'll be waiting for you, you know—if you ever come back."

I grabbed her, kissed her, and patted her rump. "I'll be back, sweetness. Don't worry. Just rest up."

She came with me when I went to buy the duck trousers and blew kisses as I was taken shipwards by the silent sailor in the sea beret. I felt sorry to be leaving her. I really liked the baroness. I promised myself I'd come back with a

59

whole skin and spend at least a week with her before taking the TWA jet stateside.

When she was a tiny speck on the beach, I turned and stared at the *Athena*. This would be my new home for a week or two or three. It was a magnificent sight, all white modernity.

I had seen only a glimpse of her interior; I knew she had a big lounge where the guests assembled to play games or just talk, an adjoining bar, and a dining room capable of seating more than a dozen people. I did not know all the details at the moment, I learned them later; but I was impressed with its size, the sleek shape that disguised that size to the eye, and with its overall elegance.

I went up the boarding ladder to the sight of a pair of tanned, slim legs under a striped bikini walking along the deck. The legs paused. A hand lifted a long strand of yellow hair so that a pair of deep blue eyes could assess me.

"What ho?" a childish voice asked.

It was no child who faced me in the bikini and rope clogs. No top; the breasts that confronted me were as tanned as the legs.

I made a little bow, remembering my status. "Allow me to introduce myself, miss. Rod Damon, your new steward, at your service."

A pouting mouth smiled lazily. "They got rid of old Wrinkle-cheeks, did they? Well, good for Georgey-porgey."

"I believe Emile has retired. He's gone back to Paris."

"Goody. You, we can have fun with. You're young, more or less. Just how old are you?"

I smiled mechanically and bowed. I pushed past her and walked toward the office door. She turned on a sandaled heel and snapped. "You, there. I spoke to you."

My feet went on walking. I thought she might come after me to make a scene, but she did not. I wondered if I had made an enemy. If I had, the hell with it; I did not like pampered brats who pushed.

Georges Fortescu was sitting at his desk when I walked in on him. He was a big man with dark black hair graying at the temples. He wore a turtleneck black sweater under a white blazer ornate with gold braiding. He looked like a rough customer in a fight, his knuckles were big, swollen from old breaks. Instinct told me this Greek businessman had been in many a free-for-all before he had accumulated his uncounted millions.

His black eyes lifted to stare at me.

"Damon? The new steward?"

"Yes, sir."

"I imagine Emile told you your duties."

"Some of them."

He smiled frostily. "You'll learn the rest. Keep your nose clean and we'll get on fine. Your pay is two hundred dollars the month. I'll have Alex brief you on what we expect of you. That's all."

I made a little bow. I was at the door when Fortescu spoke again. "Damon, remember one thing. I have a boatload of—ah—jet-setters. A couple of movie starlets, some very rich, important people. If they want—ah—special attentions, I assume you're man of the world enough to know what to do?"

I grinned. "I like to think so, sir."

Georges Fortescu laughed. It transformed his hard, craggy brown face into something human and likable. "Good, good. Then we understand one another. Good luck!"

I went out into the Riviera sunlight. The sailor in the striped jersey had swung my valise and carryall onto the deck. I lifted them and started walking. A maid in microskirt and frilled uniform blouse with an equally frilly cap on her brown hair, flirted with me as she showed me where Emile Crillon had bunked.

She also told me my next duty would be to attend the dining room, to take orders for drinks, to supervise the service, to be at beck and call.

I went into the room and closed the door behind me. I unpacked my things. There was a tiny closet that held about half of what I had with me, so I kept the rest in the valise and shoved it under the bunk. I lay down and crossed my ankles, staring up at the white ceiling. I dozed.

When I woke, the *Athena* was under way. Its twin

61

motors were throbbing faintly, deep in its bowels, and there was that surge underfoot that let you know the ship was making good time as it headed eastward past the Côte d'Azur.

I dressed in white ducks, blue blazer, white shirt and tie.

If I was going to be a ship's steward, I would be a good one. I went up the companionway to the main deck, finding my way into the bar. A small, older man was turning on the bar lights. I nodded, introduced myself, and studied the bottles and the equipment. The man stared at me almost hopefully.

"You know liquor?" he wondered, after a moment.

"I know liquor. I want to see how well you're stocked. You have pretty much of everything you'll need, I should imagine."

The bartender, whose name was Andreos, nodded gloomily. "I guess so. I do what is ordered. I try to make cocktails for these people. I do not do so good. They make the funny faces."

I enjoy making friends. I said, "Tell you what. If I get the chance, I'll make the drinks. How about it?"

His relief was almost comic. "The family, they usually drink only wine. And wine I know. But these others, these jet-setters, they ask for crazy things. Martini. Manhattan. Robert Roy. Who knows those?"

"I know them, Andreos. I'll make them happy."

I was at the doorway when they came in, the women in evening gowns, the men in dinner jackets. I bowed; I escorted them to their chairs; I answered their questions. Ilona Fortescu beamed when she saw what an impression I made. Even her husband seemed in more of a jovial mood.

The snotty blonde babe I had met on deck was named Fleur Devot, a starlet in a French movie company. There was also a French banker and his wife—Alain and Celeste Maillot—a Spanish manufacturer, Eduardo Herrara, with a lovely brunette whom I realized at first glance must be his mistress, though they called her his secretary, Juana Batione. Add to these a handsome male movie star, apparently the boy friend of the snotty blonde, a dancer named Donna Romminet, a second blonde who was quite

62

obviously her own particular friend, Barbe Serrelle, and you know the guest list.

The Fortescus ordered wine, the Maillots requested martinis.

My blonde friend was gleeful as she opened her eyes wide and asked, "Might I have a Pimm's cup?"

I overcame the urge to belt her one and made my stewardish bow. "Anything, miss. What base?"

She looked a little blank. I don't think the little tart had ever had a Pimm's cup in her life; she'd just heard the term.

Patiently I explained, "There are six basic Pimm's liquors, miss. Which one would you prefer?"

Celeste Maillot smiled happily, saying, "He has you, Fleur. Admit it, you haven't the faintest idea what he's talking about!"

Everybody laughed. Fleur Devot went white with fury. Her boy friend, Pierre LeMoines, whinnied with laughter like a horse. I figured she might haul off and belt me, or demand I be set ashore at the nearest port, so I made an even deeper bow.

"There are Scotch liquers, gin, rye——"

"Gin," she said hastily. "Make it gin."

"*Moi, aussi*," intoned her boy friend.

"I'm going to change my mind, Rod," murmured Ilona Fortescu. "I believe I'll try a Pimm's cup myself. But make mine Scotch."

"It will take a little time to build one," I warned.

"No matter. We'll chat," smiled Celeste. "And include me on the Pimm's cup. It's been ages since I've had one."

I went to the bar. Andreos looked on with wide eyes as I foraged around until I found stemmed glasses large enough for the Pimm's cups. I selected four, I began to build them with the gin or Scotch bases, the soda, the added fruit. A Pimm's cup can be a work of art. I made mine into artistic perfections. I added an extra one for myself so I could sip it and make certain the others were as delicious.

It took me ten minutes to make them properly. Beside the Pimm's cups, making the martinis and the other drinks was nothing. I set the glasses on the trays and made my way back to a serving table.

I placed the drinks and stood back.

Inside moments, I was being overwhelmed with compliments. Even Fleur Devot admitted that hers was *trés bon*. Georges Fortescu took a sip from the straws in his wife's cup, nodded after smacking his lips, and eyed me with new respect.

"What jewel have you come up with, Ilona?" he murmured. "A man who knows how to make drinks? Incredible."

"The best martini I've had east of New York," added Alain Maillot.

The compliments flowed in. I stepped forward after a while to take the dinner orders with something like confidence inside me. I figured maybe I could pass myself off as a steward, after all.

The girls in their mini-skirted uniforms served the pâté de foie gras mousse and scampi grilled over charcoal as hor d'oeuvres, pressed duck with gigot d'agneau or galantine of duck as a main dish. The diners finished up with a Chantilly cream cake for a dessert.

The serving girls and I would eat later.

It was a little past ten when they left the table. I was starved. I did not help clear the table; that was not my job. I just walked into the kitchen, sat down, and reached for what was left of the leg of lamb—the gigot d'agneau—that was so heavily stuffed with kidneys, mushrooms, truffles and flavored with Armagnac. I ate like the famished man I was.

When I was done, I turned to the chef who was undoing his apron. "Armand, *le bon Dieu* is waiting for you to die to make you head chef in His kitchens."

Armand beamed.

I took a stroll on deck. I knew my duties were not at an end, a steward is on call at almost any time of the day or night, especially a steward like myself, who was the only one on board ship. But I wanted a little time to myself. I am not used to catering to the whims of a dozen people.

Ahead of me, I saw a slight figure leaning against the rail. As I came closer, I recognized the pert little French maid, Angelique. I was about to speak to her when she gasped and stiffened, moving back a step from the rail. She had been staring out to sea. I turned my eyes where she had been looking.

A man was treading water, staring at the ship.

"*C'est impossible!*" she cried.

We were ten miles out into the Mediterranean. No man in his right mind would be swimming this far from shore. I felt a cold, premonitory chill ripple down my spine. A merman? But as Angelique said, it was impossible.

The man dove, disappearing.

Angelique was shivering. I put an arm about her, frightening her almost as much as had the sight of the swimmer. When she recognized me, she pressed closer, shivering.

"Could it be, what I saw? A man?" she quavered.

"Some men are mad—*tres fou!* They fancy themselves as athletes. He was a night swimmer, no more."

"But there are no ships around. Look for yourself. And nobody can swim so long underwater. He hasn't come up yet."

"It may be war exercises of some kind," I told her. "He is probably an aqualunger, attached to a submarine. The submarine is beneath the surface. It is night; perhaps the crew is practicing ejection in case of an emergency. The *Minerva* sank not too far from here, you know."

"Yes, I suppose so. But it was scary."

She was a pretty little thing, young and friendly. I told her to go to her quarters and forget what she had seen. Angelique seemed to think that was a fine idea. I watched her coat swing from side to side as she crossed to a deck door and opened it. Her fingers wriggled a farewell at me.

I went on pacing around the deck. I was worried, frankly. The man we had seen had been no submariner. There had been no diving equipment on his pack or head. He was a merman. I was positive of it.

But in that case, why was he shadowing the *Athena*?

There may have been a submarine, one of those small undersea craft that hold two men, below us. The submarine could be paralleling our course. The swimmer had emerged to make certain ours was the ship they wanted to trail.

65

Once certain of that, they could keep after us, unseen, just below our keel or behind it, utterly unknown to anyone on board ship.

Should I tell Georges Fortescu?

I decided against it.

The next few days at sea were utterly unexciting. I was up to attend the breakfast party, I brought deck chairs, I put on a mini-brief and served as a lifeguard when the guests donned swim trunks and bikinis to cavort in the waters off Sicily and later, in the Ionian Sea that extends from the boot of Italy to the Peloponnese.

I had expected more fun and games on this cruise. Maybe all the excitement went on behind closed doors in the guests' cabins. I had very little to do and my time was my own between breakfast and dinner, outside my duties as lifeguard, which gave me my chance to get the Mediterranean sun and plenty of exercise, swimming here and there in the blue waters.

My health was never better. As a matter of fact, I was almost too healthy, if there is such a thing. The hot sun, the blue waters, the excellent food, the lazy days on deck watching seven nearly nude girls and women swimming around in the Mediterranean, was affecting my gonads.

I was on deck the fourth night after leaving St. Tropez when I saw a merman for the second time. It was not the man I'd seen off the Côte d'Azur, this man had a bald head, and much broader shoulders. He came very close to the *Athena*, as if he did not care whether he was seen or not.

I was alone at the time. I watched him for a few minutes as he swam alongside us, gradually falling behind as the yacht continued its steady ten knots an hour. Then he dove and disappeared.

We were a dozen miles offshore. To our port side, in the distance, I could barely make out lights on the island of Kythira. There was forty miles of open water on our starboard side, as far as the nearest land, which was the island of Crete.

This time I reported what I had seen.

Georges Fortescu ridiculed my eyesight at first. "Nobody can be swimming this far out to sea without scuba

66

equipment. You must know that, Damon."

"Yes, sir—except for a merman."

He jumped a foot and stared at me coldly, suspiciously. He muttered. "A merman? You mean like a mermaid?"

I told him a little of what I knew about the mermen. We were in his office. I'd interrupted him leaving the main lounge after more cigars, and the door was closed behind us. He had taken out half a dozen cigars, now he paused while inserting them in the sterling silver case he carried in his dinner jacket pocket.

He waited patiently until I was through. Naturally I did not tell him it was the baroness I saved. I made up a name for a nonexistent female. But the fight with the mermen, and how I killed them both, I related with exquisite honesty. It seemed to me his face got darker and more menacing, the longer I talked.

"Extraordinary," he murmured when I was done. He pushed the cigars into the case and clicked it shut. "If this is true, it deserves some publicity. Have you told anyone about it—besides me?"

"Not yet, no," I lied.

He beamed his pleasure. "Good, good. We'll talk about this tomorrow, Damon. Do me a favor—don't tell any of my guests or crew what you know. We'll keep it a little secret between us, shall we?"

I agreed to thaat as I had no reason not to, but I did not tell him that Angelique had seen the first swimmer. His reaction to the news disturbed me. He should have scoffed more or been more alarmed. He was quite calm about the shole thing and did not seem at all surprised.

The next day went by uneventfully. The ship was calm and quiet. The guests ate and swam and loafed in the Aegean sunlight as they had been doing. There was an undercurrent of excitement among those guests, however, a sense of something about to happen, that touched my personal alarm system like a dentist drill does an exposed nerve.

Maybe I should have listened to this personal alarm system, which I have developed to a nicety since my employment as a Coxeman, but I enjoyed the hot sunlight and the swimming as much as anyone. I found the opportunity to belt down a couple of martinis before dinner. I floated in an aura of pleasure with the guests.

I did not realize how close we were to Thraxos.

However, I did wonder at Georges Fortescu. He had not sent any radiograms to the authorities inquiring about mermen swimming in the Aegean Sea. As the industrialist he was, and with the guests he carried on board—all of them fine candidates for possible kidnapping and ransom—he ought to have been more careful. The least he could have done was make inquiries. To my certain knowledge, he did nothing.

I was puzzling over this while strolling about the deck after dinner next evening when Ilona Fortescu came out to join me. She was wearing a black satin evening gown that clung to her slim middle and full hips and showed off much of her mature breasts—which the panels that formed her low-cut bodice did little to hide. I had not seen much of Mrs. Fortescu during the voyage, other than at mealtime and when she had swum in the sea. Frankly I had been a little disappointed in Ilona Fortescu. She had promised much with her eyes, that first afternoon I had seen her breasts, but nothing had happened between us, so her sudden request surprised me.

"Rod, would you be good enough to draw my bath?"

I followed her swaying hips across the deck and to the door of her stateroom. I knew that she and her husband had different staterooms, but I had not given it any thought until this moment.

Her stateroom was decorated in pinks of assorted hues, and a chalk white. Her bed was canopied, coverleted in pink and white taffeta. The floor was carpeted from wall to wall in the same pink. A long closet adjoined her bedroom on one side. On the other, there was a roomy bathroom done in blue and white delft tiles.

I walked into her bathroom, letting my eyes roam over the double tub with its sterling silver fixtures. Old-fashioned carriage lamps on the walls added the final touch of pampered luxury to the lavatory.

68

I turned the silver faucets, I tested the temperature of the water. I laid out towels and the perfumed soap Ilona Fortescu favored.

When I turned toward the open bathroom door, I started in surprise. Ilona Fortescu was lifting her black satin evening gown upward. I stared at the handsome legs she displayed in black nylon stockings. She had excellent legs, slim but fully curved. When her soft bare thighflesh came into view above her stocking vamps, I cleared my throat.

As if remembering my presence, she turned and smiled at me. She did not drop her skirt, she kept it at the level of her upper thighs, an inch below her privacy. The sight of those superb stockinged legs affected me like an aphrodisiac.

"Yes, steward?"

I smiled back at her. "If your husband should come in right now, Mrs. Fortescu, he might misunderstand the situation."

Her laughter rang out. "My husband never comes into my stateroom uninvited," she assured me.

I could see the way her eyes ran up and down my own body, settling at the pronounced protuberance at my loins. Her eyes grew very bright, and I thought that her breathing quickened.

"I should have asked Angelique to draw my bath, I suppose," she murmured, "but the poor dear is indisposed. You don't mind this, do you, Professor?"

"I enjoy it, madame," I assured her.

She hesitated, then murmured, "Angelique sometimes stays to wash my back for me. I suppose I couldn't ask you to do that, not in your clothes and all."

"If madame would permit?"

I took off my jacket blazer, folding it across a chair arm. I undid my tie, I removed my shirt. I kept glancing at her from time to time, seeing that she was taking an extraordinary interest in my strip act. I put my hands on my white ducks and raised my eyebrows.

Mrs. Fortescu nodded, so I slipped the trousers down and stepped out of them. All I wore were thin shorts that

69

failed completely to cover my male excitement. My employer stared in undisguised admiration at what she saw.

"Olisbos," she whispered, blinking.

"Priapism," I nodded. "It's an affliction of mine."

She lifted her eyes to mine for a moment, before dropping them to this olisbos that so intrigued her. Her voice murmured, "Affliction, Professor? Surely you misname your problem."

I shook my head. "Unfortunately I do not. Priapism—or satyriasis—is a medical anomaly. When I become excited, I can find no relief."

Like the baroness, she was disbelieving. She even laughed a little. "No relief? Nonsense! Why, I myself can furnish all the relief you need. Which is to say," she added coyly, "I have the potential to do so."

"You're a very beautiful woman, Mrs. Fortescu, but no woman in the world can help me. Believe me, I have tried."

She interpreted this, as all women do, as a challenge. I could see the glint in her eye, the firming of her jaw, the tightening of her lips. She felt my words to be an imputation upoon her femininity.

Her hands lifted her evening gown higher, to the level of her navel. Under it, her hips were concealed in a black girdle. She wore no panties, and the dark thatch of her womanhood was visible between her fleshy upper thighs.

"Show me," she breathed. "Take off those ridiculous shorts."

I pushed them down. She gasped and her eyes grew wide. Her hands tightened on the black satin, her body wriggled, and the evening gown went up like a curtain rising, showing me her heavy breasts flowing out of a black lace brassiere, quivering gelatinously despite their confinement as she lifted the gown off over her head. She brought her arms down, letting the black satin dangle from her fingers as she stared at me.

The room was silent. We could hear the gurgle of the water sliding past the hull as the *Athena* slipped through the Aegean Sea. We were traveling at night; we had our riding lights on; we were well beyond the Sea of Candia between Crete and the Greek island of Santorin by this time.

Suddenly I heard sounds on deck.

Shrill cries and the thudding of feet, the slap of a hand on flesh, the deeper voices of excited men; we could hear them in the stateroom as if they were just beyond its door. Ilona started and turned her head a moment toward a porthole, staring, scarcely breathing. Then she turned back to me.

"We must hurry," she murmured. "Come, undress me."

She turned her soft, creamy back, bisected by the strap of her brassiere. I came up behind her, so close that she could feel my excitement nuzzling at her soft thighs. She was panting harshly, head thrown back a little. I could feel her thighs move against me.

"Please! Please hurry," she whimpered.

At the time, I did not understand the reason for the hurry. The boys and girls outside on the deck were having themselves a time. They would not rush in to interrupt us. My only worry was her husband, but she had assured me he would never enter her room without a specific invitation.

The brassiere cups drooped as I unclasped the strap. I was peering over her shoulder as I had on deck the first time I had set foot on this yacht, but now we were alone. I was free to indulge the caresses which I knew she would enjoy. I kissed her bare shoulder with my open mouth and ran my lips up to her soft throat.

My hands slipped along her ribs to her swollen breasts. I slipped my palms over them and held them gently. Just as gently I began a bouncing movement, up and down, up and down. I reached for her turgid nipples. I fondled them, rotating them between my forefingers and thumbs. Unable to stand my teasing, she turned and plastered her front against me.

Ilona Fortescu was panting like a bellows. Her hips swung; her thighs opened to fasten upon my body; her girdled hips bucked and looped.

"Aiiie!" she wailed, thighs tightening their grip, and driving her breasts against my chest, clinging to my upper arms with her hands as she dragged her stiffened brown

71

nipples back and forth against my chest hairs.

She was unwittingly performing the rite of *tekhfidz*, as the Arabians call it, which is the brushing of the male member back and forth between the labia minor, in a form of mutual pleasure between man and women. The Latin terminology knows it as *penem fricatum inter femorum*. There is no penetration, there is only the excitement of both male and female erogenous zones, which leads, by its very intensity, to a mutual orgasm.

Ilona Fortescu held me in a painful finger grip; her eyes were squeezed shut; her lower lip was caught between her white teeth; her head hung back, moving from side to side as if she was caught in the coils of a epileptic fit. She was unable to control the agitated movements of her hips and thighs. Her physical side had taken complete command.

I was nudging her backward, toward her bed——when someone screamed in agony outside the cabin wall.

The sound ran through us like a knife in butter. Ilona jerked back, the motions of her hips stilled. Her eyes popped open and showed me the stark terror inside them, through which the glaze of pleasure was slowly fading.

"What is it?" she panted.

"Never mind that. They're having a party, deckside."

"No. You must—go see!"

Her hands pushed me away. As if she was suddenly ashamed of her actions, she turned and ran toward a closet, reaching inside for a chenille robe to throw about her girdled nakedness.

"Go see, go see," she begged.

"Like this?"

"Your ducks—put them on. Please, Rod."

I shrugged. The intense pleasure I had been enjoying was still in my nerve ends. I felt like a starving man dragged from a feast. I knew rage and a sudden weakness. I was frustrated and furious at the same time.

I climbed into the white ducks, I slid a shirt over my chest. I pushed feet into socks and shoes. Ilona Fortescu was huddled beside her open closet door, staring at me with wide eyes.

"I'll be back," I promised.

72

I went out into the companionway, closing the door behind me, and I could hear the laughter and the shouts more clearly. Men and women were yelling, screaming in an orgiastic excitement. And a girl was screeching in utter terror, in a fear that was riddled with white-hot agony.

I ran.

I came out onto the deck to the sight of what seemed to be an orgy out of a voodoo cult. On the deck, tall candles were glowing, illuminating the stark naked body of the pretty little maid, Angelique. She was writhing and twisting to the hands that held her down on a valspared hatch coaming. Her face was contorted with fear and revulsion as she stared upward at a flopping chicken in the hands of the ship's cook.

A knife was being drawn across the chicken's neck.

Eduardo Herrara had planted himself between the widespread legs of the maid whose ankles were gripped by a couple of the crewmen. As the knife sliced into living flesh, he drove himself forward into the screaming girl.

Angelique jerked, screeching like a lost soul.

The knife ran cleanly into the chicken and blood gouted downward across her heaving breasts and belly. The people massed around the hatch moaned and screamed in answer to the double blooding, for the maid had been a virgin. Vaguely I was aware of throbbing drums, as I told myself she might have been the only virgin on board.

I stood frozen for a moment, not believing what I was seeing. This was voodoo all right, from the cabbalistic candles to the rada drums. I remembered suddenly that there were voodoo cults in Paris, and ceremonies to which the initiated might bring guests.

Angelique was flopping about almost as much as was the decapitated chicken. Her screams were punctuated by the laughter of the onlookers and the shouts of sensual joy Eduardo Herrara was making as he violated her body. The candlelight, the shadowed faces of the onlookers, the blood streaming across the white flesh of the raped girl, was like something from a psychedelic nightmare.

I came out of my paralysis slowly.

The intense surprise of seeing a voodoo rite performed

73

on a yacht deck in the waters of the Aegean Sea had held me rigid. Too, the sight of Herrara driving himself with metronomic rhythm into the body of the screeching girl probably touched some sadomasochistic chord deep in my own being, keeping me from interfering earlier.

I was vaguely aware that the guests of Georges Fortescu had joined the crowd of *loa* worshippers and were themselves participating in the orgy. I recognized Celeste Maillot, maturely curved in black brassiere and nylon panties and high-heeled shoes, her diamond rings flashing on her fingers as she moved them, and beyond her, the Spanish dish, Juana Batione.

Juana displayed no jealousy for what her man was doing. She was bent forward, loose black hair falling in a spill of ebony past her heavy white breasts, her entire body stark naked above her shoes. A crewman was beside her, his hand moving across her plump buttocks, making them jiggle as she stared at the voodoo rite.

The blonde dancer, Donna Romminet, was pressed against her lesbian friend, the icy brunette with the almost painfully thin body and the oversized breasts, caressing those breasts with frantic, nervous hands, as they both watched what was being done to Angelique in something like hypnotized horror.

I made out Alain Maillot with his arm about two pretty waitresses, grinning from ear to ear as he held them tightly to his unclad body. Neither of the girls wore a stitch of clothing. Even their feet were bare.

Then I came out of it.

"Hey," I yelled, lunging forward.

It was a mistake. No sooner had I taken two steps then the men all whirled and hurled themslves upon me. In a corner of my mind, I know this had been rehearsed. Nobody acts that fast to an interruption. It was as if the entire tableau had been planned with one fact in mind: to get Damon!

I ducked under a fist and grabbed an arm and used the *gumura*—the major wheel throw—to hurl my first attacker into the air so that he went flying across the deck and into

74

the chest of a second man. Somebody leaped on my back. It was a woman; I could feel her hard breasts pressing into either side of my spine as her perfumed forearm went about my neck and hooked my throat. A fist came out of the lights to drive into my belly below my belt buckle.

I went backward off my feet.

My body was like a piledriver slamming into the soft body on my back, that hit the deck with a sodden thud. The woman screamed with pain in my ear. I rolled off her, kicking upward into a male crotch and listening to the man echo the screech of the female.

I rolled over and over, driving into a pair of naked legs and upending the woman in the bra and panties—Celeste Maillot—angling her fall so that her hurtling body took a husky crewman out of the action. I came to my knees throwing punches at three men driving for me. My fist met a jaw. The knuckles of my other hand slid off a shoulder.

Then a body rammed me backwards.

I hit the deck hard with a muscular crewman on top of me. I surged upward, trying to throw him off, but somebody kicked me in the head with a foot. The foot had a shoe on. I saw more stars than there were in the night sky overhead.

A knee rammed my middle. The breath whooshed out of my lungs. I tried to turn on my side but a fist was catching me across my jaw. The back of my head bounced on the deck planks.

"Don't kill him," a woman yelled.

"We want to have our fun," a girl shouted.

Fists and feet hit me, again and again. I bucked and grunted to the force of those blows. I hurled a fist; I sought to knee a man, but the fury was gone out of my muscles. A man stood over me, and as strong hands held my wrists and ankles, he drove a bare foot into my belly. I tried to double up against the pain shooting throughout my body; I could not. The men who held my wrists and ankles were too heavy to move.

The foot hit me again. Again. Again. . . .

Nobody could take a pounding like that and not lose

consciousness. I was no exception. I went away into a blackness for a few minutes, where it was quiet and peaceful.

The peace and quiet did not last.

I came to on my feet. Somebody began yanking off my clothes until I was standing there in front of everybody, stark naked. I was dizzy, sick. My body ached from the beating it had sustained, and my middle seemed to be a voice telling me how badly it had been bruised.

Hands pushed me stumbling backwards until cold wood and metal touched my spine. I was being shoved into the mast. Then ropes were flung around me, tightening at my belly and my thighs, being wrapped about my arms that were drawn behind me. Fingers were knotting the ropes on the other side of the mast.

A crewman was moving about with a pail of cold water, dumping some of it on the faces or heads of the men I had knocked out. I watched these bruisers shudder, shake their heads, lie there on the wet deckplanks, gasping and groaning. I felt a little better when I saw the damage I'd done.

There was respect in the faces of the men, and something like awe in the eyes of the women as they gathered around me. Georges Fortescu was there, puffing on a cigar, smiling wickedly at sight of my helplessness. In the shadows beyond him, I could make out his wife, Ilona, in her chenille robe.

"Sorry about this, Damon," Fortescu said slowly. "You were a good steward, the finest we ever had."

Fleur Devot was giggling uncontrollably, trying to stifle her laughter with both hands. "Tell him, Georges, tell him what we are going to do to him!" she was crying between bursts of gleeful laughter.

"In good time, Fleur. There are some things I want him to understand first. He is a *flic*—a police spy sent to report back to the authorities about what we are doing on my little yacht."

This was a blatant lie. I knew Fortescu knew I understood it, because he winked at me slowly. I began to grasp the situation.

Georges Fortescu was a S.E.L.L. man. One of the mem-

76

bers of that Secret Enemies of Liberty League which battens upon the fears and intrigues of world powers. Let someone find a new weapon or a new chemical formula, and S.E.L.L. will beat a bloody path to his door, to steal his invention from him and offer it to the highest bidder in the world market.

As a Coxeman, I have fought S.E.L.L. before. I have been shot at by, and I have killed, S.E.L.L. secret agents. If S.E.L.L. was interested in the mermen, I knew why I was being set up for the kill. I had seen mermen following the *Athena*, I had reported my discovery to Fortescu, who was a S.E.L.L. agent. Therefore, I must die.

I wondered about men and women like Fleur Devot, Celeste and Alain Maillot, Juana Batione and Eduardo Herrara, and all the other assorted guests. They could not all be S.E.L.L. people. Or could they? Maybe this *Athena* was a S.E.L.L. possession, and all of its people were on a semi-holiday, on their way to the Greek island of Thraxos where they would be briefed on the sales pitch S.E.L.L. would use to auction off its discovery to the world power most willing to pay its price.

In any event, knowing all this was doing me no good at all. They were going to kill me, here and now, on the foredeck of the *Athena*.

But—how?

77

CHAPTER FIVE

The beautiful blonde dancer told me.

She came striding naked across the deck, a thin bamboo rod in her hand, sadistic glee in her eyes. Georges Fortescu drew back to give her room. She lifted her right arm, far back, then brought it forward. The thin rod came down across my belly, just above my manhood.

"Nnnnggggl!"

It was not a scream. My teeth were clenched, my tongue was curled up in my mouth, I could only make that sound deep in my throat, my every muscle strutted against the agony eating in my flesh. My head rammed back into the mast, my body came up on its toes.

"Man," Donna Romminet sneered, like it was an insult.

The rod drove into me again, across my loins. This time I could not help it. The pain was too intense to fight. I threw back my head and howled out my agony.

Donna laughed harshly. "Scream, scream all you want—man!"

The bamboo rod lifted and fell, lifted and fell. It whipped my manhood, it flailed my flesh until I knew I was bleeding like a stuck pig. I was half out of my skull by this time. I kept flopping and hopping on the deck plankings, trying to get away from that rod that was trying to make a eunuch out of me. I could not look down to see the damage that was being done; there was a rope across my throat, so tight as almost to choke me, which kept me from lowering my chin.

I could only imagine what my manhood looked like, and

78

my imagination had me in shreds. I had never felt such pain. I hoped I never would again.

The blonde lesbian would have killed me all by herself if left to her own devices, but Georges Fortescu made a gesture with a hand and two crewmen came up behind Donna, caught her bare arms and yanked her away.

The thin bamboo rod was covered with blood.

I wanted to die.

"Naughty girl," Pierre LeMoines said.

The handsome young movie actor came forward with a bowl and a soft washcloth. He sat down at my bare feet and began to inspect me.

"She left you in a pretty bad way," he muttered.

He lifted the washcloth, soaked in oil, and began to wash my bloody flesh. Some of the others watched, but off to one side I could make out through the red haze that swam before my eyes, the sight of Barbe Serrelle kneeling before the sobbingly excited Donna Romminet, red-nailed hands clasping her soft white buttocks, arms about her thighs, kissing the shaven flesh of her inamorata, while the blonde stood with spread legs, head thrown back, eyes wide open but unseeing as she stared blindly upward at the stars.

The hands at my bruised, bleeding flesh were curiously gentle, almost as if they wanted to repay me with pleasure for the pain Donna had caused. He almost crooned to himself, seated before me.

He laughed suddenly, looking up at my face that was held fast by the rope around my throat. "I'll bet you thought you were going to have a ball with Ilona, didn't you? You didn't know she was setting you up for us, did you? To let us get the stage ready. You're our star performer, you know. Oooohh, and you really are a star!"

"Five stars, Pierre," whispered Ilona Fortescu from behind the actor.

"You should know, darling," breathed Celeste Maillot, leaning to rake my chest with hr fingernails, not roughly enough to draw blood, but enough to hurt. Her eyes glistened with excitement. "Was he fun? Did you have enough time for *cracher*?"

79

I was writhing to the touch of the oil-soaked cloth when Celeste pushed Pierre away. "Enough! It is my turn to torment him. *Ma foi!* I have never seen anyone so formidable!"

Celeste knelt down naked before me, kissing my toes. Her fingernails ran up and down my thighs, very gently. It was very pleasant, her kissing. It sent a chill of desire down my spine that settled in my manhood.

Ilona whispered, "*Sacré bleu!* He is growing even more, Celeste!"

The lips creeping up an ankle said, "We shall kill him with the torments of the senses, dear Ilona. We shall make him burst a blood vessel, yes? We shall rupture him with *rivancher,* as Chinese courtesans used to kill a man with the torture of the thousand caresses."

Lips and a wet tongue on my thigh, moving upward. Bright red fingernails sliding before them, scratching lust into my every neuron. I twisted and shook, I felt the delight gorging my blood vessels with tumid power. The mouth moved open-lipped across my thighs to my belly, bypassing the straining flesh that practically begged for release.

Celeste was a past mistress at this titillation of the senses. Her teeth nibbled, her tongue licked, her lips ran wetly here and there. Where her lips went, there went her long fingernails. My teeth were biting my tongue against the pleas trembling on it. I wanted to ask for relief; I wanted to beg for satisfaction; I felt I had been teased enough.

Now she was crouching, kissing my belly, my chest, running her tongue across my nipples. Upward to my throat went her lips while she pressed her breasts to my ribs, adding to my delighted discomfort. Always she avoided touching my straining, tormented manhood. If I had not been so excited by Ilona Fortescu, I might have been better able to resist the pleasure she was giving me. As it was, I struggled against the ropes that held me. I tried to fight back the flesh-fire in my veins. I sought to pretend I was having none of it.

Fool that I was! My distended member gave the lie to that idea. I was afraid something *would* burst in my veins.

Celeste was hoping for just that happening, as her voice crooned to my ear, as her nipples scratched my chest, as her fingernails trickled teasing torture on my quivering thighs.

She drew back, eyes bulging slightly in awe. "*Mon Dieu!* Look at it! I have never seen anything so huge."

"Except on a horse," giggled Fleur.

Juana Batione was beside her, long black hair flooding down across her pale shoulders, hiding her heavy breasts. Her skin was so white as to be almost an abnormality, but it was sensually exciting on the Spanish girl. It made you think of girl slaves kept in a harem for the sport of their master. Only her lips and fingernails were red, the rest of her was all white skin and glossy black hair.

The Spanish girl said, "I am next."

She turned and ran, soft white buttocks jiggling. I heard a soft whine, an excited bark. Juana reappeared tugging on the collar of a big German shepherd dog. Her laughter at the expression on my face was raw, wild.

"You shall see something that will drive you crazy," she laughed. "And you shall watch—or I will have Donna beat you some more where it hurts so much."

She straddled the big dog, rubbing herself against its bristly fur, squatting down on it as if it were a mount. The dog must have engaged in such activities at other times, because its lust was evident. It whined pleadingly and squatted on the deck until Juana cuffed it, making it stand upright on all fours. She drove herself back and forth on the animal until she was hunched forward, head hanging, her pallid breasts swollen and her hips moving like a metronome out of control. She made an exciting picture. If I had not been bound like a sheep for the slaughter, I would have torn her off the dog and raped her.

I must admit I did have one thing going for me, all through my ordeal. I possess a little of what the psychologist calls mind control. I was able to employ self-hypnosis to keep my physical body in check, to hold my own lusts in abeyance. I could look at what the Spanish girl was doing and not let it affect me as much as the others, for instance, were being affected.

81

I have studied hypnotism. I have learned a little of the method of mental domination of the senses. The mind possesses a strange control over the body; it has been scientifically demonstrated that the human brain can change actual physical results, as when a hypnotized man demonstrates that he can walk even though his legs have been anesthetized; as when he will eat a blotter and enjoy it, believing it to be a steak; another man, believing he was being fed honey, actually had the sugar content of his blood rise! If such things can happen, surely the mind can blank out pain. The North American Indians are believed to have possessed this ability to autohypnotise themselves and so endure stoically the frightful tortures their enemies heaped on them at the stake. When a Mohawk Indian did, so did I.

So I hung there in my ropes and endured. I could not control the evidence of my own arousal; I was not adept enough for that. But I could alleviate the suffering I would otherwise have endured by keeping a tight rein on my emotions.

The shipboard guests were not so well controlled. I could see Georges Fortescu with his arms about the hips of the naked blonde danseuse, who was bent adoringly between the parted thighs of her lesbian inamorata. Fortescu was driving himself like a living piston, while the danseuse, sandwiched between the man and the woman, was striving her utmost to please them both.

To one side of them, Pierre LeMoines was caught in the grip of plump white thighs as Ilona Fortescu bucked and rammed in unison with his thrustings. Her bare back was pressed down on a blanket spread across the deck planks. Her eyes were shut but her mouth was open as she gave out soft little cries of pleasure.

There were other bodies, other men and other women here and there in the shadows, indulging the desires that had been born of my torture. One or two of them were watching Juana and the dog, turning their eyes toward me, even as their love partners worked savagely to bring them to their orgasmic release.

Juana was kneeling before me, smiling. Her hand

caressed the dog, the animal whined and jerked to that fondling, nuzzling its cold nose between her thighs.

She said, "Sport is a good dog. Good dog. He has been well trained. He cost a lot of money, you know. No, Sport—down. The time is not yet."

Her black eyes glinted up at me. "You know about lap dogs, hey? I know you are a teacher of sex in America. So you know about this. But have you ever seen it?"

They call it bestiality, this relationship between a human and an animal. It is not a new vice, by any means, it has probably existed since there were men and women and animals. In Roman times, women condemned to death were often raped by beasts first, to slake the sadistic thirst of the Roman audiences. Specially trained animals were employed for these tasks, just as they are today at sex shows in the capitals of Europe, in Mexico and in North Africa, where dogs and jackasses are so employed.

It is quite common on farms, for there young boys and girls are exposed to animals, and form attachments to certain pets. And world explorers have told of native women who have taken apes for their husbands, and will not mate with a human, preferring the performance of their hairy companions.

Juana Batione was spread out on the deck, legs wide. Her dog was busy pleasing her flesh with his long tongue, so that her body jumped and jerked from time to time, and her soft red mouth gave out little yelps of happiness. It was a sight to stir the lust in male veins. It stirred mine, and came close to making me lose my control.

Soft female laughter mocked me from the deck where the Spanish girl lay shaking. She cried, "You wish you could be where the dog is. Admit it! You are wishing I would be as nice to you."

I felt as if I were in a nightmare. I fumbled with the ropes that held me, I twisted and writhed back and forth. It seemed to me that the knots were loosening; the ropes that held me did not seem as tight. I tried to catch a knot in my fingers, but it kept eluding me.

While I worked at the knot, Juana turned over and rested on her knees and elbows. She reached behind her for the dog, guiding it. Then the animal was at her, and her wail of pleasure punctuated the night.

I wondered where her boy friend was, the rich Spanish manufacturer. I tore my eyes from her bobbing hips long enough to scan the deck. I saw Eduardo Herrara engaged with the lesbian friend of the blonde dancer, Barbe Serrelle. He was kneeling between her thighs, kissing her as Donna Romminet had kissed her, and making her enjoy it just as much.

Juana was screaming before me, slapping the deckplanks with her palms as she crouched down, slave to her animal passions. I wondered what quirk of character had turned her to this divertissement instead of toward a man. Lucius Apuleius in his Golden Ass tells of a rich matron who enjoys the love-making of a jackass; I suppose Juana Batione was sister under the skin to that lady.

A shadow fell across her white back. Fleur Devot was standing, grinning down at the wailing woman and the dog.

"One side, you two. Your act has lost its charm."

She reached out and touched my belly gently. I could not help the convulsive jerk that was the answer to her questing touch. She laughed softly.

"These others—they are pigs," she whispered. "They know only the enjoyment of the physical senses. They aren't subtle. They know what arouses them, and they think the same thing arouses everybody else!"

She was very close to me. There was perfume—Joy, I think it was—in her blonde hair, and a very wise devilment in her blue eyes. She licked her lips, staring down at me. Fleur Devot was the essence of everything that was erotic in the world. She had tiny breasts, but her nipples were extremely long, and at the moment, in a state of excessive length. Her belly was almost flat, dimpled by a sunken navel. On either side of her shaven pubes, her thighs were tanned columns of curving loveliness.

She kicked the dog in the flank. "Move. Go on. Move!"

The Spanish girl began to crawl on hands and knees along the deck, dragging the German shepherd with her. Fleur laughed.

"Poor Juana. She cannot help herself. She's quite unable

84

to cure her little problem. Eduardo indulges her pranks, of course. He thinks she is great fun. She puts on exhibitions for him and his friends. She gets girls to help her entertain them. I understand she's helped swing half a dozen million dollar orders for his company."

Fleur smiled like a fallen angel. "They are gross, all of them. No imagination. I've been watching you, you know. You are excited, yes. But you're nowhere near dying from that excitement. And those others—pouf! They have not the control. They get hot and they let go with their lusts."

She began to laugh. "What a joke! *Them* trying to kill *you* with sex! It is they who will do the dying first. But me, I have a different idea about you. I think I shall try it out. I shall appeal to your mind, to your imagination, instead of just to your physical senses."

She turned and fled on bare feet across the deck toward a pile of clothes hurriedly thrown alongside a winch when the deckside orgy had begun. Her fingers lifted a shoulder bag, fumbled inside it. Then she brought out one of those giant lollipops that one buys in the sweet shoppes. She held it up and waved it at me.

She came back and seated herself yogi fashion before me. Her slim brown thighs directed my eyes toward her shaven privacy. Giggling, she put out her tongue and began to lick the lollipop up and down.

Fleur tapped me with the lollipop, getting me sticky. Her voice was a low croon as she said, "You understand the symbolism, my dear professor. Your mind won't be able to run away and hide, because the symbolism will appeal directly to your mind and to your imagination.

She put the lollipop to her mouth, taking as much of it as she could into that yawning red cavity. Above the sweet at which she nibbled, her eyes were gleeful. I guess she could see how she was getting to me with her lollipop love. It was oddly wicked, more exciting even than the act Juana Batione and her German shepherd had put on.

Her tongue ran up and down and around the sweet. She slurped its taste in between her lips. Her mouth worked all around its edges. She licked and licked, devouring the goody as if it was the first one she had ever tasted.

85

To seek a crutch to help me against the sight of her little-girlness showing itself off to me, I caught hold of the knotted ropes and tightened my fingers on them. I hung on for dear life, telling myself not to let this blonde starlet do what Celeste Maillot and Juana Batione had been unable to do.

A red tongue lapping, soft red lips enclosing, sharp white teeth biting ever so gently, to tenderly, into the sweet. Mouth open, mouth moving slowly all over it. Saliva painting those wet lips even redder. The moving head, bobbing back and forth, the fingers that held the stick of the lollipop, gently squeezing.

My own fingers tightened on the ropes spasmodically. I strutted my muscles in a vain attempt to overcome this clever, calculated appeal to my mind. I have trained myself to watch couples as they enjoy the copulative embrace and to be unaffected by the sight; it is part of my technique as a teacher of sex and sex techniques. I had not trained myself to ignore this more subtle appeal to the lusts that live deep in every man and woman.

I groaned, staring down at her.

Fleur laughed, delighted at the success of her stratagem. With just the tip of her tongue, she licked the edge of the lollipop. She ran it back and forth, under and over. She was a girl devil. She knew damn well what she was doing to me.

She paused long enough to whisper, "It gets to you, doesn't it? It stabs you where you live. I know. Once a man tied me up with my legs wide open and sat between them, eating a peach. It nearly drove me insane." She pouted, leaning forward to examine me more closely. "But my body helped me, as yours is not helping you. My body spent and spent its juices. But yours does not."

No need to tell her I could not. I was in no mood for a lecture on satyriasis. I just wanted out of this dilemma.

She put the lollipop into her lips again.

And a rope yielded to the tug of my hands. I could feel that give, as the rope loosened where it bound my arms behind me to the mast. I ran my fingers along the rope to the knot, discovering that the knot had also loosened.

I worked on that knot with quivering fingers. The ropes gave a little more. I was learning that one big knot served to keep the rope about my neck and my arms about the mast behind me. A different knot had been used to tie my ankles to the mast.

I tried to be discreet about all this. I wanted to surprise Miss French Starlet in the middle of one of her licks. She must have thought all the moving around I was doing was because she was exciting me beyond endurance.

The knot fell away just as Fleur Devot was taking the lollipop out of her mouth to speak. She got as far as, "Now let me rub——"

I lunged, figuring the movement would loosen the ropes at my ankles sufficiently for me to pull my feet out. It did.

Fleur started to scream as my body dropped on her.

She never made a sound.

Both my arms locked tight about her shoulders as I drove my open mouth down on her lips. Another part of me drove hard into her femininity. I went in to the hilt. My tongue tasted sweet lollipop, that other part of me tasted a deep moistness that sent bolts of electricity up and down my spine. Fleur rolled over on her back. I went with her.

The little bitch had been orgasming steadily, teasing me. Even so, her womanhood was tight and narrow. My gigantic size must have hurt her deeply, because her body stiffened and her head went back with convulsive fury as she tried to scream. My tongue and mouth blocked her yell, so that it was a deep, throaty whine that sounded in my ears. My hips pounded my manhood at her deeply.

She was fighting me, but my strength and size was too much for her. She made me think of the tiny girl-priestesses the high priests raped before their gods, Baal and Ashtoreth, in the days before Moses led the Habiru out of Egypt. I felt like one of those bearded Canaanites with a girl-priestess in my arms. My blood boiled, my heart hammered. I worshipped the lustful goddess and her consort, deep in my heart. This female had teased me beyond endurance. I was going to have my vengeance on her.

I drove like a drill hunting oil. I bounced her bottom off the deck planks at every thrust. I gave her every last bit of the Damon priapus and I damn near split her in half. She yowled; she howled; she tried to claw me, at first. But I noticed that after a minute of this steady pumping, in some sadomasochistic way, the pain became a pleasure to Fleur Devot.

Her hips still bounced and bumped as we inched along the deck, but now it was a rhythmic bumping, a combined convulsion of chaotic carnality. She was grunting in my ear and her slim arms were straining my hairy chest against her enlarged nipples, she had got a leg lock around my hips and her heels beat a tattoo on my behind, like she was riding a horse and spurring him to greater speed. At least, that's the way I chose to take it.

"Don't stop, oh, never stop," she sobbed.

Her fingernails bit little arcs in my shoulders where they clung to give her body greatest leverage. She was biting my chin, kissing my throat, keeping up a steady humming sound deep in her chest. This little blonde starlet was away out there in love-land and she didn't give a damn who knew it.

A voice whispered, "Come on!"

It was not a female voice, and it seemed to come from the water itself. I thought: If any mother's son tries to pull me away from this piece of French tail, I am going to strangle him with my bare hands, because I had been caught up in the swirl of the same sexuality that enthralled Fleur Devot; like her, I was hung up somewhere in Paradise. I drove and thrust, and I was received and cradled deep in her loins.

I gave to Fleur Devot what I had had for Ilona Fortescu, for Celeste Maillot, even for Juana Batione. I freed myself of the sexual tensions of an entire night in this single driving madness.

A hand touched my shoulder. A third hand, not one of Fleur's; hers were still digging nails into my flesh.

"Get the hell away," I snarled.

The hand went away. Something cold and metallic replaced it. I have been serving the Thaddeus X. Coxe Foundation long enough to know the touch of a revolver barrel on my neck when I feel it.

"Goddammit, aren't you human?" I moaned.

Somebody chuckled sympathetically. "All right, all right."

We were somewhere in Nirvana, the little blonde and me. We were coming down the stretch neck to neck, and the finish line was there with spangles all over it. We would hit it together.

Her hips leaped; mine dropped.

She screamed thickly, head flung back. I bellowed down at her open mouth, seeing her eyes like white slits through the long golden lashes, smelling the Joy and the feminine odor of her at the same time and wanting to merge my flesh with her flesh.

We quivered together for long moments.

"Oh, my God," she whimpered, staring up at me.

Thre was awe and happiness and a strange submissiveness in her eyes. I bent and kissed the corner of her lips.

"Thanks, honey," I breathed.

The gun tapped my shoulder, "Okay, now?" a voice asked.

I slid out of the saddle. I turned my head.

A man in a black rubberoid swimsuit stood grinning at me. He held a revolver in a hand, and the revolver was aimed at my navel. His head jerked.

"Over there. With the others."

Sometimes I react very slowly. I turned my head and saw Celeste and Alain Maillot with their bare hides on, crowded in against Pierre LeMoines and Donna Romminet, with Barbe Serrelle just beyond them. The maids were there too, all of them stark naked, even little Angelique, whimpering in pain and doubled over. They had all been taking part in the mass orgy on deck when I'd come out of Ilona Fortescu's stateroom.

There were other men on deck, all of them in the black swimsuits. They had no scuba gear, just the rubberoid garments to withstand the chill of the cold Aegean waters. The man with the revolver aimed at me lifted his left foot and kicked out at me.

The kick never landed. I grabbed his foot, twisted it,

sent him crashing off balance down on the deck planks. I dove off the deck toward the snub-nosed Belgian Bulldog he had dropped. I got my hand on it, hit the deck and bounced as I tried to turn around in mid-leap.

One of the mermen was coming for me, fast.

I aimed off the cuff. I triggered the Bulldog.

The merman died in mid-air, a lead pellet in his brain. The others came for me in a body, guns out and aiming. I would have died there, if it had not been for Georges Fortescu.

"No, no," he shouted. "I want him alive!"

I had forgotten Fleur, who had been spreadeagled on the deck when I pulled out of her. She had sensed what was happening, she had slithered around behind me—for protection, I thought at the time—and now she hurled herself at me, grabbing my right forearm and biting deep into my gun wrist with her white teeth.

The pain was sharp, numbing it. At this moment I couldn't have shot my cuffs. I yelped and tried to swing her away.

"Idiot," she panted. "I'm saving your life!"

I felt something hit the back of my head. I fell forward, out cold, into a blackness shot with red lights. I swam around in that blackness for a time, then my head cleared and I opened my eyes.

I was looking at a pair of bare feet. Girl feet, attached to girl ankles and shapely girl calves. I stared up at dimpled knees. The knees bent and the rest of the girl came down toward me.

It was Angelique. Her face was twisted in a grotesque mask of pained sympathy below the fall of brown hair that tumbled to her bare shoulders. There were traces of tears on her cheeks.

"Are you all right?" she whispered.

"I guess so. What about yourself?"

Her face crumpled up and I think she would have cried if I hadn't caught her hand and squeezed it, saying, "Don't give them the satisfaction, honey."

She drew a deep breath and nodded. I took advantage of the nod to scan the rest of her body below her chin. For a

90

recent virgin, she was stacked mighty well. Her round breasts with their rather large nipples quivered only slightly to her movements, while her soft white belly made attractive creases in her kneeling posture.

I put my hand to the back of my head. No, no blood. I tried to sit up and Angelique helped me, gripping my left wrist and getting to her feet, pulling me upward. I swayed a little, I leaned against her, standing on the *Athena's* deck.

She felt good to the touch, her body was soft, cushioning. Against my will, my manhood told me it liked her too. She felt it grow against her thigh, but when I expected her to draw away thinking I was just another beast-man set on ravishing her, she surprised me by making a crooning sound deep in her throat.

"There, there. It'll be all right," she breathed.

"Poor kid," I whispered. "I should be the one comforting you. That was a hell of an experience you had tonight. Still hurt?"

She nodded her long brown hair against my chest. I told her, "If I had some medicine, I could take care of you. What's going on here anyhow?"

I looked around the deck. Angelique and I were alone for the moment. The rest of them—guests and the invading mermen—were at the starboard rail, looking out across the moonlit waters of the Aegean. There was a motor humming, faintly off to one side.

"They're sending a tender to pick us all up," Angelique murmured.

"Prisoners of S.E.L.L.," I nodded.

"Hein? What's sell?"

"Tell you later, honey. Just for now, let me relax."

She giggled suddenly, moving her thigh against my clamoring manhood. "You must move away from me. Otherwise, you will never relax."

I grinned down at her, delighted to see that she was not shrinking away from me, as any recently raped virgin might be expected to do. I drew her a few steps backward into the darker shadows and turned her so her front faced mine.

Angelique gasped then, and pulled free. Her dark eyes under their long lashes questioned me.

"You know the first thing they do to an aviator who's had to jump from his plane? They make him take another one up, right away. Or to a man who's almost drowned? They make him swim as soon as he recovers. It's therapeutic treatment, it gives a man back his confidence. I think I ought to prescribe that for you."

"I hurt too much," she whispered.

"There are ways," I assured her. "Besides, we can't go anywhere until that tender gets here."

"You are mad!" she exclaimed, but she also giggled.

I put my hands on her curving hips and drew her slowly forward until she touched me with her lower belly. I did not hurry her, I let her feel the strength of my manhood gently pressing into her. She quivered and her tongue came out to run around her somewhat overlarge red mouth.

I waited, knowing damn well that her healthy female body would like what it was feeling, and that the sensory excitation she must be experiencing would be as good to her bruised flesh as any ointments I might apply.

She began to rub herself against me slowly, like a frightened fawn nibbling at a sweetmeat. I just held her hips, I did not urge them forward or back. I let her do what she wanted. I remembered what Ilona Fortescu and I had done in her stateroom. Angelique would not go so far, I was confident. Instead of the *tehkfidz,* she would be satisfied with the *sehhq kelbet el-mes'hhuq* of the Egyptians, which is the rubbing of the male organ against the clitoral bud of the female.

This method of sexual pleasure is a great favorite in the coffeehouses and inns of North Africa. There, grown men consort in this manner with the little girls who frequent these *funduqs* in their desire to learn sexual techniques which will prepare them for their future lives as prostitutes. There is no penetration, there is only the exquisite pleasure of the sustained caress.

I admit I was not all that altruistic. I was letting the little French maid enjoy herself because I hoped the pleasure she received would make her look more kindly on men in general, and help her forget her recent rape, but I also was getting a bang out of the proceedings myself.

Her soft hips locked to mine, moving gently and then faster and faster. She was clinging to my arms with her hands, her eyes closed and her teeth sunk into her lower lip. As her movements increased—I was aware of the pressure of her rigid clitoris by this time—she opened both her eyes and parted her lips, gasping.

"Ooooooh! Ooooooh!" she breathed.

"You see? Sex is a beautiful thing between a man and a woman. It is a God-given gift to all human beings." I felt as if I were on the podium, lecturing a beginner class in my League for Sexual Dynamics. "The trouble is that it's perverted by some men and some women into something bestial."

She was melting against me, letting her hardening breasts know the firm musculature of my chest, moving them up and down even as her hips pumped wildly against my manhood. She bucked and she moaned. When she was about to collapse from the delight that swam in her flesh, I put my arms around her and held her.

After a time, she stirred. She kissed my chest. She whispered, "I never realized what my body could mean to me. And you taught me."

"Now, look."

Her soft palm covered my lips. Her eyes stared up at me in utter adoration. I began to think that I had made myself an ally against what was to come.

"Don't say anything. Please," she begged.

So we stood like that, pressed into each other, while the tender purred closer and voices sounded at the starboard railing. A rope ladder was being lowered. I watched Celeste Maillot throw a tanned bare leg over the rail and begin her descent.

A merman turned from the rail to look across the deck. Before he could raise an alarm at our absence, I hooked my arm about the little French girl and stepped with her out of the shadows.

"We're here," I called. "I was just a little woozy."

Georges Fortescu turned at the sound of my voice. "I'll want to question you, Damon. Barbadonis, keep your gun on him."

The merman named Barbadonis lisped, "I thurely will."

I did a doubletake at the big merman. In the moonlight, his body appeared softer, more curved than it should. I noticed his motions seemed almost feminine. I scowled, trying to get my facts straight. It appeared that these mermen went in for homosexuality. I had to think about that. It might put a new light on what I was going to find on Thraxos.

Because I was sure we were going to that little island. I had been following our course toward the Dodecanese islands, and I was reasonably certain the *Athena* was at anchor now some miles off Thraxos. It was almost dawn and there was a hush on the world. I sensed the ghostly presences of ancient ships with their sails spread to catch the wind, bound on some eternal voyage across the wine-dark seas of Homer.

Angelique pinched me.

"Sorry. I was daydreaming," I muttered. "Maybe it was the blow on the back of the head."

The merman smiled at me. And he scowled at Angelique as he waved his revolver, gesturing us to the rail.

We clambered down into the tender. Me first, because Angelique said she was afraid and wanted me to go first down before her, so in case she fell I could catch her. I took one glance down at the tender, seeing the Fortescus guests all wrapped up in blankets against the morning cold, including Ilona and her husband, and a few of the crew.

Then I looked up as Angelique flung a leg over the rail. I kept my eyes on her full white buttocks as they jellied to her descending legs. She was a dish, this little French girl.

A hand tossed me a blanket. I drew Angelique against me and wrapped the blanket about us both. We sat down together on a thwart, crowded up against Donna Romminet and her girl friend, both of whom gave us daggerous looks.

Ilona Fortescu said, "I see our Angelique has found herself a protector."

Her husband grinned, "He won't be a protector for long. He's a prisoner, and we keep prisoners in jail."

The tender moved away from the *Athena*, its sharp prow

94

cleaving the blue Aegean waters. A handful of crewmen remained on board; I could see them lining the rails, watching us move away.

Angelique was shivering. I held her nakedness tighter to my own. I felt like shaking myself. I was going into the S.E.L.L. lair without a weapon, without even so much as a shirt to cover me.

I wondered what was going to happen.

CHAPTER SIX

The island of Thraxos was a purple swell in the Greek dawn as the tender moved toward it. Legend said that Helen of Troy had stopped here with Menelaus of Sparta, her husband, on their way home from Troy. There was an ancient roadside shrine high in its hills that gossip claimed she herself had built to the goddess Aphrodite in gratitude for her rescue from the Trojans.

For more than a thousand years after that, Thraxos had lain in a little back-eddy of Time. Not until the Knights of St. John set up a small port there, and a tiny citadel to protect it against the attacks of the Saracens, did it again enter the main stream of history. The Hospitalers had made a valiant stand against the Turks in the sixteenth century, but they were forced to give way to overwhelming numbers. They sailed away and never came back.

Today Thraxos dozes in the sun, almost forgotten by the world. It possesses three towns, the largest being Pelagayos. It is inhabited by fishermen and their families, as are the two smaller towns on the north side of the isle. The harbor at Pelagayos is small. It holds a dozen fishing smacks and a ketch or two.

The tender slid into the harbor between two stone moles projecting outward from a stone quay lined with shops and houses. Several rows of houses, white against the darker bulk of the small mountain behind them, with red-tiled roofs, were a pleasant sight in the rising sunlight. The thought touched me that the harbor and the houses made a disguising facade for whatever S.E.L.L. was doing on Thraxos.

Two small buses were waiting for the Fortescus and their guests. We moved by ones and twos out of the tender onto worn stone steps half sunken in the harbor water. Angelique would not leave me, she clung to my hand, her troubled face turned up to mine.

The buses chugged along a dusty road, curving onto the mountainside and bypassing the white stone houses. Here and there a man or a woman paused to stare at us, hands across their foreheads to shield their eyes from the sun. One woman, seated atop a jackass, laden with goods for market, waved a hand and grinned a toothless smile at us.

Over the mountaintop we went—past the weathered stones of a wayside shrine, possibly the one Helen of Troy had caused to be raised—and down the other side. We could see the dark olive trees in their groves, the fields of white and yellow wildflowers, an occasional farmhouse with its goat corrals. It was a pleasant sight in these early morning hours. I could have enjoyed a vacation here, say, with little Angelique as my companion.

The sun rose higher in the sky. We were approaching the western shore of the island, where a natural bowl had been formed with one side flat and open to the sea, perhaps in some long-forgotten time when Thraxos had been a volcano. A compound of modern buildings loomed ahead of us, tastefully fitted into a background of gnarled olive trees and the ever-present flowers; to the west, the vast blue Aegean glittered in the sunlight.

This was S.E.L.L. headquarters, its laboratories and dormitories, on Thraxos. A wire fence ran all around it, except where it faced the sea. There was one gate, before which our buses braked as Fortescu leaned from his seat behind the driver and waved a hand. The gates opened and the buses drove through.

In the distance I saw two men walking, their arms about each other's waists. They were strolling as women stroll, their hips swaying from side to side. I began to wonder what was what around here.

The buses pulled between the buildings, we were ordered out and into a small bare room of a long bulding. A merman—I assume he was a merman, though he was

97

dressed in a sport shirt and very tight slacks—brought us clothes to wear. Angelique dropped her side of the blanket right before his eyes, standing naked and unconcerned as she bent for the mini-skirted maid's uniform which she was to wear.

"Hey, honey, remember your maidenly modesty."

Angelique giggled. "He isn't interested in me. It's you he's looking at."

He was, too. I folded more of the blanket around me, saying, "I'm straight, mac." He shrugged, smiled, and left without a backward glance.

"Are they all like that?" I wondered.

Angelique paused with her uniform half over her nudity to shrug. "All the ones I've seen. Why?"

"I'm not sure," I said thoughtfully. "I hadn't figured on anything like this. It adds a new facet to my problem."

The mini-uniform was down about her hips. Her white legs were exquisite in their shapeliness. I stared at them as she brought the wide collar of the maid's outfit down past her tousled brown hair.

"I don't think there'll be time," she giggled, seeing where I looked.

She was so right. Almost instantly a small loudspeaker tucked into a ceiling corner began to blare.

"Attention, all guests. You will assemble in five minutes inside the auditorium, which is the round building at the center of the compound. Any merman will give you directions."

Angelique pushed her black uniform down past her naked hips, making a face at me. "It begins now."

"What begins? How much do you know?" I slapped my forehead with my palm. "Stupid me! You're a maid, you've waited on the Fortescus. You must have heard something of why we've come here like this."

She was turning her pale back for me to hook her up. I bent and kissed her between her shoulderblades as she said, "I never heard much. A few words, more or less. They're here with their guests on a kind of holiday. For kicks. There was also something about childbirth, but I can't remember what."

"Childbirth?" I yelped.

"Yes. They want children here, I understand. Why, I do not know." She squirmed as I kissed down her spine. "Do you hook up all your girl friends this way?"

"Only the ones with irresistible backs."

I did up the fasteners. I had more on my mind than a French girl's smooth back at the moment. If the mermen were concerned with childbirth, maybe they were interested in an underwater city, and in women they could alter into mermaids. But I had it all wrong.

As Angelique and I emerged from our bare little room into a concrete walk, we saw the guests hurrying toward the auditorium. We started off side by side, but a merman intercepted us.

"You will please come with me," he told me.

I blew the girl a kiss. "See you later, honey. Keep your chin up and your legs down."

The merman gave me a dirty look. In some ways he reminded me of Donna Romminet, who hated men, except that I think this merman hated women. He gestured me ahead of him along a branching walk.

The walk lead to a red door. The merman opened it and moved back for me to precede him.

We stepped into a metal chamber fitted out like an operating room. Glass walls surrounded it, forming a narrow corridor which went past it into a larger room that looked like a hotel lounge. A man was seated on a divan, browsing through a newspaper.

When the merman told me to halt, I did.

The man put down his paper and smiled at me. In his late fifties, he was tall, with hard Germanic features. The crewcut hair on his head and the hairs of his Van Dyke beard were shot with iron-gray. There were creases at the corners of his mouth, and a sleeping bitterness lay deep in his hard blue eyes.

"*Ach,* the Amerikaner. Good! I wish to talk with you. Georges Fortescu tells me you are a spy of some sort."

"Georges Fortescu is a liar," I lied.

The man smiled. He said, "Permit me to introduce

99

myself. I am Herr Doktor Ernst Bachmann. I am a biochemist."

I bowed a little. "I've heard of you, herr doktor. You're internationally famous."

He smiled with real pleasure. "Ah, you have heard of me? Then you will regard what I am to tell you as the truth, not as the maunderings of some harebrained mad scientist from a Grade-B movie. I am the man responsible for the mermen I understand you saw in the water while on the *Athena.*"

He rose to his feet, slim and immaculately groomed. He ran a hand across his beltline and frowned. "For some years now we biochemists have been experimenting with what might be termed chemical engineering. We have been trying to better the Creator's own work by improving it. We seek to make men over so they can live underwater. Why do we do this, you ask?

"In the year 2000, the world will not be a fit place in which to live. There will be an estimated five billion people living on our planet, and not enough food can be produced to feed them all. So then, where do we go? Not to the planets, because there isn't any which could be safely colonized in such a short period of time. When then, you ask?

"I say, into the ocean."

He was walking up and down with crisp, short strides. His right hand moved here and there in the air as if he wielded a baton to beat out the rhythm of his speech.

"In the ocean. *Ach*, yes. Have we not already been thinking along such lines? Some years back, two Frenchmen lived thirty feet beneath the surface of the sea in a kind of bathyhouse equipped with beds, stoves, television and electric lights. What they could do—could two hundred million? Maybe. But is there time to build a big enough complex to house them all?"

"I have come up with the answer. I shall adapt mankind to the sea, not the sea to mankind. It is good thinking, *ja*? You might call this a branch of the cybernetic engineering which has been going on now for more than a decade. In a sense, we are trying to rebuild people to live in a new and completely different—even antagonistic—environment.

100

Bionics, of course, gives us a hand here, a science in which we seek to imitate nature by studying the eyes of the frog, the ear of the owl, the gill of the fish.

"Ha! The gill of the fish. Could man imitate that, then he could very easily go underwater, build vast cities below the surface of the ocean. He could extract the oxygen his body needs from the water all about him. There would be rest-stations floating on the ocean top, of course. There, men and women could relax and breathe in proper amounts of oxygen which might be denied them by the ocean.

"And hydroponic farming—now being carried out so successfully by crews of nuclear submarines—might become a giant industry. Perhaps we must turn to the oceans to raise food to feed all the people in the world at that time. Farmers who could breathe underwater might well be the answer to the overpopulation problem."

I cleared my throat. "You make sense, herr doktor."

"*Danke!* All biological organisms such as man, beast and fish, are really nothing more than electrical systems reduced to flesh and blood. Eh? *Gut!* Between man and fish there is only the difference in the manner in which they get the fuel—the oxygen—they need to run their systems. Man gets it from the air, the fish from water. Can we give man the ability of the fish in this regard?"

"You can," I nodded.

He glowered at me as if I had insulted him. Then I realized he was glowering at himself, not at me, for he said, "*Ja, ja.* I have done that, but I have made a mistake. A most vital mistake. I have turned these men into—but come!"

He drew me with him toward a large picture window covered by a draw drape. He grasped the pull-cord and yanked.

I was staring into a lounge, part of this tremendous compound of interlocked buildings. I gathered it was a one-way mirror on the other side.

There were only men in the lounge, I realized, though many of them were dressed as women. Transvestites. They were rouged; their bodies were displayed in the most modish dresses; they wore stockings and high heels. A cou-

101

ple of them were even making out with some of the men still dressed in slacks and sports shirts.

"Bah!" snarled the doctor.

"I don't get it," I muttered. "How come you go for the gay set when making your mermen? It would seem to me——"

"The gay set? *Nein, nein.* These men were as masculine as you—before I put my special sea-serum into them. This is the mistake, you see, the drawback that may well end the human race.

"For the sea-serum upset the hormone balance in their bodies, kills off the male hormones, enables female hormones to grow and take over. The result, you see. Every merman is a fairy!"

His laughter was bitter as he drew the drapes closed.

"Poof! There goes my hopes to become a kind of Poseidon, a sea god who has given the human race another dimension in which to dwell. How can those—things —procreate? Oh, I have given it a lot of thought. I have no answer. I am defeated.

"Perhaps!"

He accompanied this last word with an odd look at me. The short hairs on the nape of my neck stood up, and a cold chill rippled down my spine. I lifted both hands.

"You aren't putting that serum in me, doctor!"

He actually smiled. "*Nein, nein.* My need for you is in another direction, a happy one, if you are the man I think you. Because, you understand, I have made some new discoveries. By injecting baby mice, I find the individual mouse retains its male characteristics up to and through maturity. You grasp the implications of such a discovery?

"If I could have human babies to inject immediately after birth, these male babies would grow up to be real mermen. They would not be homosexual. They would be all man male."

"And you need babies," I murmured.

"*Ja, ja!* With strong, healthy fathers!"

My mind reeled for a moment. Me—the father of the future human race! Me, Adam. Then I remembered I'd had a vasectomy operation some time back. A vasectomy pre-

102

vents a human male of mature age from becoming a parent by preventing the flow of male semen through the vas deferens, the duct which carries this fluid from the seminal vesicles.

I decided I would not tell herr doktor this fact. It would cut off my supply of available females, I was sure. It might also cut off my life, since he might no longer need to keep me alive. So I pretended to be overwhelmed with the notion. The doctor assured me it was no idle brag of his. He was fully capable of doing what he said he could.

"Have not others before me pioneered in this field of biochemistry? In your own United States, scientists have made an android that has a heartbeat, a pulse, and blood pressure. His eyes dilate, his chest moves as he breathes. I advance the study a few steps farther. I take the living body, I administer the proper chemicals that will create a change, I make the true merman."

I grinned. "And all I have to do is make the babies."

"*Ja, ja.* This is not hard work, *nein?*"

"Well, in one sense it is, doctor," I replied. He did me the compliment of chuckling at my wit, then became serious again.

"I must tell you a little of this vaccine which——"

A gunshot sounded. I heard the voices of women yelling. I turned toward the archway into his laboratory, but the doctor was ahead of me. He was running fast, so I ran after him.

We came out into the sunlight on a cement walk and into view of what seemed to be a mob of angry women. They came pouring out of the round auditorium in screaming groups of threes and fours. They were shaking their fists in the air. A couple had knitting needles they were sticking into the mermen racing out ahead of them.

I saw Georges Fortescu go down under half a dozen screeching, scratching females. He was trying to protect himself with upraised arms, crying out that he was not responsible for what had happened.

"*Gott in Himmel!*" breathed the doctor. "I was afraid of something like this! We have got to shoot them all, all those crazy women."

103

This went against the grain. I was staring at a pair of luscious white thighs revealed under a mini-skirt. I saw a women with a torn blouse out of which a pair of ballooning breasts had burst to bobble up and down very provocatively. Another girl had her skirt up above her bare behind to give her greater leg freedom while chasing a fleeing merman.

I couldn't let the doctor kill all that lovely female flesh.

"Hey, girls,". I yelled.

A redhead in slacks and sweater lifted her head. She stared at me, then yelled, "There he is. There's the bastard!"

"Look," I yelled, "I'm no——"

The woman wheeled and came for me. I started to turn and run when I saw Fleur Devot in a jersey dress coming up fast on my flank. "Not you," she called. "They mean the doctor."

Ernst Bachmann was fleeing for his life. I saw my opportunity. I ran for him, left my feet in a diving tackle. He crashed onto the cement walkway pretty hard. As a matter of fact, I skinned an elbow and a knee myself.

Next moment the women were all around us.

Their red-nailed fingers clawed for the doctor, who tried to shrink under me. I lifted my hands and bellowed.

"Take it easy! What's all the excitement?"

Half a dozen voices tried to tell me all at once. I gathered that most of these chicks had been brought here for fun and games. They had been promised husbands and a good living. Unfortunately, by the time they got here to become wives or mistresses, as they chose, the sea-serum had changed healthy males into healthy fags who wanted no part of any female.

They had just been briefed on this tragedy by Georges Fortescu, whom I gathered was Ernst Bachmann's second-in-command. Naturally, since their emotions and their libidos had been raised to explosive levels, they had blown their valves and revolted.

I was standing by this time, crowded in by a dozen or more warm, soft girl-bodies. One of the girls was even giv-

104

ing me a rather personal feel, and discovering that I was no merman, by any means.

She announced her findings in a gleeful chortle. "Girls! Look!"

I felt cool air around me. I was really exposed now. The girls all flocked around, fingering and admiring my manhood. They were out of their skulls with excitement, the whole lot of them. Their expectations had been built up so much that their maidenly modesty was a thing of the forgotten past.

"Hold everything!" I roared.

"I'm trying to, honey," a brunette dish giggled.

"That's not what I mean. Listen. Listen. Now calm down and let the doctor up. I think he has a plan to announce that will please you all."

Hands dragged Bachmann off the cement. His face was scratched and bleeding. His scowl told me he considered me a traitor. But he talked fast enough as the women crowded in, threatening to mutilate him.

"*Ja, ja!* What he says is true. I have been considering your situation, and I have a solution to offer."

He told them his solution, which was simply that I was going to impregnate them all. Or try to, anyhow. Some voices scoffed that no one man could do that.

"Then we shall go out and capture more men," Bachmann yelled. "We have the means to do it. We shall send the mermen out and——"

That was a mistake. The girls swarmed in around him, yelling that the mermen would keep the captives for themselves.

I thought fast. I said, "I offer a different plan. You shall become Amazon abductors yourselves. You can go raiding the island villages for young, healthy specimens of manhood. How about that?"

They liked it.

"What about the mermen?" glowered a redhead.

"We'll work something out," I told her. "Now let's go back to the auditorium and talk this whole thing over."

"Not yet. We want guns!" A blonde screeched.

Bachmann had the keys to the ordnance building on him. He was hustled along to that building and forced to open the locked doors. The women helped themselves to Luger automatics and holsters, to Russian AK-50 automatic rifles and bandoliers fat with bullets. They really did look like Amazons when they came out.

"What's your name, honey?" the redhead asked.

"Rod Damon, lady."

"Rod?" screeched a Frenchwoman. "*Roide* in French means penis. And how better could you be named?"

"King Roide!" yelled a blonde.

"King Roide! King Roide!"

They would have lifted me to their shoulders if I had not fought them off. "Look, girls! Let's be sensible. Let's go talk this over in the auditorium."

I walked ahead of them like the king I had been called, but I made myself more modest, much to the dismay of my female followers. I was thinking fast. I had the opportunity to blow this S.E.L.L. setup sky-high and I meant to do it, but my better judgment told me I couldn't go about it too quickly. After all, I was kind of a prisoner of these over-sexed Amazon babes myself—even if they did call me *roi roide*.

I led the way into the plush-seated auditorium. I dragged Bachmann up on the stage. A dozen women acting as my personal bodyguard came with us.

"Talk fast," I told Bachmann. "Offer to support them. You really haven't got any other choice, you know. There'll be a royal battle here unless you calm them down—the women against the mermen—and when the smoke clears, bang! Your great experiment is over."

The doctor was shaking in fright, but he could still think, so he nodded his head. He walked to the forefront of the stage and began to explain that his researches had shown that the chemical injections and certain types of radiation would produce true mermen.

The women listened quietly. I could see Celeste Maillot and Ilona Fortescu among them, together with Fleur Devot, who appeared subdued, and Donna Romminet with Barbe Serrelle, both of whom looked a little sick. I almost

106

felt sorry for them. They had come along on this trip for kicks, but the kicks were proving a lot too strong for their stomachs.

"You shall be mothers to the new race of mermen," Bachmann was saying. "You will live here in luxury, waited upon by servants, with nothing to do but enjoy yourselves and breed babies."

He made me think of the camps formed by the Nazis to raise boy babies for the Fatherland. I imagine Bachmann was seeing himself as a second Fuhrer. I was going along with his pitch until I could find a way to cut out of this weird wonderland and get safely away to a Coxeman rendezvous with Walrus-moustache, with Bachmann's laboratory notebooks.

If I'd had any doubts, it was Bachmann's next words that convinced me. "If there are any dissenters—we shall throw them to the sharks, eh? We shall be the new race, we shall be the gods who created it."

He was really whipping himself up into a frenzy of Hitlerism. He was seeing himself as the guiding spirit behind the cradles of the future race of mermen. Herr Doktor Bachmann was a human weathervane, able to switch courses at the slightest change in wind direction. Face flushed, he whirled and pointed at me with a quivering finger.

"There stands your leader—your Roi Roide! He shall direct you in your endeavors. He shall be a king bee —this man who shall father all your children. As the queen bee lays the eggs for the hive, so shall your king bee fertilize the ovaries. You yourselves will be Queen Bees, protected, respected, waited upon by slaves!"

He was an inspirational speaker, this Ernst Bachmann. He almost had me cheering. I know the women flipped over the idea of being mothers to a new race of humans. I guess they especially liked the part where they would be waited on somewhat like queen bees when they became pregnant. It was a wild, crazy kind of dream, but he got the women to believe in it.

There were a couple who did not believe. Donna Romminet and Barbe Serrelle were trying to push their way out

107

of the crowd to flee through a doorway. One of the armed Amazons beside me on the stage stepped forward.

"Stop those two! We can't have them getting out to warn the mermen." I guess she knew damn well what those two girls were, because she said, "We'll take a vote right now. All those in favor of being Queen Bees to King Roide raise your hands."

It looked like a forest of arms below me.

"Those who wish to be sent to safety on some other island or the mainland, raise your hands."

The two lesbians lifted their arms. So did three other women. My redheaded lieutenant said for them to come with her. She took along half a dozen armed girls to enforce her orders.

"You aren't going to kill them, are you?" I asked.

"Certainly not. We are going to imprison them for their own protection," said the redhead with a ravishing smile.

Bachmann was almost dancing in his glee, rubbing his hands together and nodding. "It is marvelous, the way it is working out. I should have anticipated the women's reactions. I am a biochemist, however, not a psychiatrist. Ah, and you, my good professor. You were perfection, the way you took over back there—saving my life. I will remember it."

"What bothers me is the mermen. What's their reaction going to be? They could throw a monkey wrench into this whole operation."

I was going along with the doctor because I had an idea in the back of my head. As king of this Amazon island, I would be pretty much the boss. I ought to be able to gather up the notebooks Bachmann kept his scientific findings in and appropriate them. Then all I'd need do would be to find some excuse for sneaking off Thraxos to a safe place.

Everything I had done so far was aimed at this goal. Everything I'd do from now on would have the same objective. So I asked again about the mermen.

Bachmann said, "They have not been aggressive. They seem quite contented with their lot. I have found them very obedient, however. They do what they are told—which is not always a feminine trait, unfortunately."

108

"We'll put it up to them," I said bluntly.

"What do you mean?"

"They can join us—or die."

After all, the mermen were S.E.L.L. agents, as was Ernst Bachmann and Georges Fortescu. I turned to the blonde girl at my elbow. She had stepped forward to take the redhead's place when she had gone off with the protestors against the planned parenthood routine.

"Where is Fortescu, by the way?"

The blonde gave me a dimpled smile. She was a honey-haired sexpot from a nearby island, I learned later, named Stella Marakza.

"He is under guard in an anteroom, your majesty," she said. "With him are the other men who came ashore from the ship."

I thought about those other men, Maillot and Eduardo Herrara, Pierre LeMoines and several of the crewmen. I would have liked to free some of the crewmen to give me a hand with the women, but I did not dare. They were all S.E.L.L. agents. I could not trust them. I was not worried too much about Bachmann; I felt I could handle him if the need arose. He was more the scientist than he was the spy. He was concerned first with his sea-serums and radiations, then with his association with the Secret Enemies of Liberty League.

I was going to have to run this matriarchal society myself.

"Okay, then—first things first. Baby doll, you come along with me. And bring about a dozen girls. We're going out to round up the mermen and give them a choice, the way we did those other girls."

"Yes, sir, your majesty!"

Bachmann blinked when I detailed two females to keep him here on the stage until my return. I think he figured that he was running the show, but he put on a good face about it, waving a hand and telling me to go ahead.

We went into the laboratory first. I gathered up what notebooks I could find, made a bundle of them, and put them in a small safe in Bachmann's office. The safe combination was in his desk. He made no secret of it, he was

109

the only one who could interpret his scientific jargon on this island.

Then we went into the lounge.

The mermen screamed and acted like the femmes they had been turned into when they saw the Luger automatics and the automatic rifles. They came along without a struggle, since none of them was armed.

I told Stella she would have to be my guide around the compound. She told me she'd love it, sidling close enough to brush one of her big breasts against me. The breast was firm and yielded only slightly to the pressure she put on it as she rubbed its thickened nipple across my arm. I put an arm about her, hugging her.

One of the other girls coughed. We broke up our embrace to go collect more mermen. We found them in their rooms, strolling through the little park adjacent to the buildings on the beach, swimming naked, and tending the various machines needed to service the compound.

We took them without a shot being fired.

Only one merman made any kind of threat. He simpered, "You just wait 'til Henriette gets back, honey. He'll do for you all right."

"Who's Henriette?"

"Actually, it's Henri Vachon," Stella whispered. "He's the biggest and the strongest of the mermen. He's off on some job or other for S.E.L.L."

"Okay, we'll handle Henriette when he gets back. Now what about guards? Don't tell me a setup like this goes unguarded?"

"There used to be guards. Lately they've been kind of lax," Stella informed me.

"Well, we aren't going to be lax. I want guards posted at—hmmm. I think I'd better learn more about this whole operation before I try assigning guards. Stella, let's hold a council of war."

We went back to the auditorium. By this time, every merman except Henri Vachon had been locked in his room. The protestors among the women were in their quarters, also prisoners. The crewmen of the *Athena* who were here, as well as Alain Maillot, Georges Fortescu and Pierre

110

LeMoines, had been placed under armed guard in the laboratory lounge.

Right now, this Thraxos layout was a priapist's paradise. And I was the priapist.

Our council of war was a gathering of me and four females. There was the redhead, Janine Karthos; my blonde Stella Marakza; Yusefa Suleyman, brunette belly dancer who had been abducted in the middle of a performance while doing a *danse du ventre* by the mermen sent to fetch women for the great experiment of Doctor Ernst Bachmann; and Theophano Linitka, a Grecian lovely with long black hair and very red lips.

I was saying, "We've got to establish some kind of law and order, you know. It'll be real chaotic otherwise. Now I'm king, and you, Janine, are my lieutenant."

"I prefer to be called the Mistress of War," Janine purred, lifting one white leg and crossing it over the other, pausing a moment so I could look up under her mini-skirt. There was a red patch between the white thighs.

As if jealous of her superior, Stella murmured, "Why not call me your sergeant in arms?"

"At arms," corrected Janine.

"In arms," repeated Stella, slowly unbuttoning her white blouse, letting it hang open so I could see the inner swells of big white breasts.

"Which leaves the position of Mistress of Entertainment to me," giggled Yusefa Suleyman, pulling her shirt up to show a moon of olive-tinted belly. I remembered, as her belly began to revolve slowly to unheard music, that she had been an expert in the *danse du ventre* in her native Turkey.

Theophano Linitka pouted, "What about me?"

"How about Chairlady of Carnality?" asked Janine.

The girls were showing their claws. I decided it was time to put an end to that kind of thing, so I rapped a hand on the arm of my chair.

"Now, now. Remember, I'm your king. And we have important matters to discuss. First of all, about the dissenters and the mermen."

"We know what to do with them," Janine smiled.

111

"You do? You mean you have a boat prepared to send them to some other island?"

"We can't do that. They'd have the police down on us," advised Stella. She was pushing back her loose blouse so that her white breasts were completely naked. Idly, she touched her rigid brown nipples with her forefingers, teasing them.

I was responding to the sight of those pale breasts, to the vision of Janine parting her thighs and slumping down a little in her chair as she brazenly drew her skirt up to her middle. She was a sight to inspire anyone except a merman. Her pale thighs were full, slightly heavy, and the shapeliness of her calves was enhanced by high-heeled shoes.

A movement to my left caught my eyes. Our Turkish delight was standing, circling her belly above the short skirt she was pushing down with her thumbs. Under the thin stuff of her batiste shirtwaist, I could see heavy breasts swaying back and forth. Her huge nipples made dark circles on her globes. When her skirt was at her lower belly, she raised her hands above her flowing black hair and began to swing her hips and revolve her belly slowly and lasciviously.

There is something intensely seductive about a belly dancer. The *sehhiqeh* of North Africa, who perform the art with the fervid passion of a rutting animal in the inns and *funduqs* that abound in Algiers, Casablanca and Marrakesh, bring to their dance something primitive and directly sexual. They are women—sometimes with a band about their loins to hide their privacies, sometimes stark naked with their breasts jiggling in a manner calculated to rouse the desires of any male in sight—who will happily bed down and perform any or all manners of copulative couplings the purchaser of her favors might desire.

Yusefa Suleyman was a *sehhiqeh* who danced to rouse a man's lust. Her olive-tinted breasts swung and leaped, their huge purple nipples pointing right at me as her dusky belly looped and jerked. Her hips went back and forth with a copulative rhythm so swiftly at times that her skirt began sliding downward past her black thatch and along

112

her soft, shimmying thighs until it reached her knees. Then it fell away completely, revealing her naked except for shoes and the open blouse.

I could not tear my eyes away from that female flesh. I did not see Janine and Theophano leap at me until their hands fastened on my clothing and started yanking it off me. I protested only slightly. What with watching Yusefa's bobbing hips and jellying buttocks, with Janine's big white breasts practically slapping me in the face and Theophano rubbing her mons veneris against my shoulder, I was like a hound straining at the leash. For a moment I wondered where Stella had gone. Then I felt my trousers being yanked down.

I expected the girls to fling themselves on my nudity, especially since they were all staring at just one place, where my flesh was paying homage to the seductiveness of the *res es-surreh* Yusefa was performing. Janine was squeezing her breasts with both hands, Stella was licking her lips, Theophano had a hand between her thighs.

"All right, which of you is first?" I asked hoarsely.

"Oh, you aren't for us," Theophano pouted.

"No, worse luck," grumbled Stella.

"We had to make a deal with the others," Janine murmured. "It was a kind of campaign promise. So that we four got to be your lieutenants, the others bargained we had to give them first cracks at becoming mothers."

Yusefa Suleyman panted, "He is good for them now. By the beard of the Prophet—will you look at that?"

Janine grabbed my wrist, yanked me from the chair.

"In there," she said, pointing at a door. "Go!"

I walked toward the door, quivering, you might say, with delight.

CHAPTER SEVEN

I walked through the doorway and found myself staring at two dozen beds lined up hospital-style against the walls on either side of the room. There was a woman in each bed. Some had donned thin nightgowns, some wore only bed jackets out of which their swollen breasts protruded. Others lay like whores, legs spread wide to show their eagerness.

They howled at sight of my condition.

A woman in the bed on my left said, "Come on, honey! Me first! We drew lots and I won." She was the daughter of a fisherman on the island of Milos, a pretty thing with loose brown hair and wide hips.

Voices raised as I walked toward her.

"Save a little for us!"

"Don't wear him out!"

"Remember, we're in this together!"

I read the fisherman's daughter like a book as she spread her sun-kissed thighs. She would not savor a slow build-up, the play of tongue and finger. She wanted rape. I hurled myself at her from three feet away. I hit my target on contact and sank deep out of sight.

The girl screeched and lifted her hips. She froze like that an instant; then I felt her shudder out her bliss. I drove at her, made her body buckle and drop back onto the mattress. She fought fiercely with her femininity, savagely devouring me, gripping my upper arms and squeezing them with all her sexually frenzied strength.

I made her convulse twice more before I swung away.

An older woman waited for me on the next bed. She was excited, but she wanted more than a fast jog. She leaned to me, caught my manhood and made an oval of her lipsticked mouth. She worshipped Priapus as the Roman matrons once had done, head bobbing back and forth. Then with a groan she lay back and lifted her plump thighs.

The others watched, of course. Their harsh breathing, their moans, the stifled curses I could catch now and then attested to the fact that they were fast reaching their point of no return. I doubt if any of them had been in on a gangbang in reverse, this way. Usually it is the woman who must service many males. Me, I did it a little differently.

From the older woman I went to a girl of seventeen, with blonde hair and a freckled face. She was the aggressor, actually. As I approached her cot, she dove off it, locking her arms about my neck, settling herself in one swoop atop my reaching member. Her hips dipped and lifted, drove and swung. I walked to the edge of the bed and let her moving buttocks sink to the edge of the mattress. I stood over her and slammed ecstasy into her flesh.

There is a legend that Hercules performed thirteen and not twelve labors. His thirteenth task was to service fifty women, one after the other, without stopping. I am no Hercules, but with my satyriasis, I thought maybe I could handle two dozen of them.

My role as the founder of the League for Sexual Dynamics demanded that I do it. Moreover, my pride as an expert in sexology required that I take each one in a different manner. Could I do it? I wan not entirely myself, I was excited beyond the point of clear thinking, with the remaining screeching, maddened females waiting for my attentions, but I was reasonably confident.

The fourth woman was a Turkish girl, plump and with olive tints to her skin, like Yusefa Suleyman. I put the back of my head on the edge of the mattress and made my naked body a living bow and arrow. My Turkish halvah-honey squealed with understanding. She lifted a leg, shot herself with my arrow, and with bare feet firmly planted on the floor and straddling my bowed body, made with a belly dance of her own.

Some of the women caught on to my plan. One of them yelled, "He's going to do it a different way with every one of us!"

"He can't!"

"He's done all right so far!"

"Hurry up, Kyra! I can't wait!'

Kyra took her own sweet time, hips jumping, grinding and bumping like a burlesque stripper. Her breasts bounced crazily every whichway as she panted and sobbed, staring down at me.

"You aren't—a man," she wailed, head back and body shaking to the fierce delight that burned in her jerking body. "You are—a god!"

"Priapus," I hinted.

Her orgasmic fury was so great she fainted, head bowed forward, body moving like a piston casing. I caught her, eased her to the floor, then stepped over her shuddering body to the pert little Frenchwoman with black hair cut in a pixie style, who laughed softly as she waited on the edge of the bed, legs up and spread.

"How weel you do me, eh?" she mocked.

I caught her ankles, drew them together and bending them far back over her head, turned her onto her side. I stabbed her at right angles to her prone body. She threw back her head and screamed shrilly, her body bucking furiously against my own. She could do little more than jog her hips in her contorted position, but she did what she could to heighten her own pleasure and mine.

Hands were touching me as I practiced *fouteur* on the Frenchwoman, since the furiously excited women who wanted me could wait no longer to take part in this pleasure parade. Fingernails scratched my buttocks and my belly, then became even more intimate. For a little while I did not restrain them, their own heat adding to my own.

But when the Frenchwoman yelled and straightened her legs, ejecting me, I felt I had to regain control of the situation. I pulled away and straightened up.

"Get back, get back!" I yelled.

A girl with tawny hair cried, "We're dying!"

I grabbed her, pushed her to the floor. I caught her legs

116

and tucked them under my armpits. She caught on. Her palms pressed the floor, she walked on her hands with my body sandwiched between her upper thighs in the classical wheelbarrow position. She was a strong girl, I walked up and down the aisle between the cots three times before she collapsed and lay satiated at my feet.

The women had gone back to their cots by this time. They were still dying with need, but they could understand that they'd get more out of their pleasure partner by disciplining themselves.

I had eighteen women yet to take.

The seventh girl was a virgin. I sensed this from the frightened but eager manner in which she stared at me and in the clumsy manner of her posture. I felt this case needed something more than the others, so I caught her face, kissed her lips, her cheeks, her eyes. I traveled down her shoulders to her breasts. She moaned then, some of her fright gone.

I kissed her soft belly as she whimpered. When my lips sought her privacy, she pushed at my head with quivering hands, but relaxed as my tongue touched her gently. The girl cried out softly in the Russian language, lying back and accepting my lingual caresses.

As her hips began to convulse, I raised myself and thrust. Her pain was slight, she locked her legs about me and clasped me in her arms. A few minutes of such new and intense pleasure was enough for her. Whimpering, she pushed me away and lay with her face buried in her pillow.

I knew that sooner or later, these women would realize that I had not spent myself within them. Right now, they did not care, they were too emotionally involved to bother about a detail like that.

"I'm next," said a familiar voice.

Celeste Maillot knelt on the edge of her mattress, pallid buttocks turned my way. "I'll make it easy for you. Try me this way," she cooed.

I caught her hips, lunged and drew her toward me. She was no novice at this game of *Venus reversa*. Her buttocks slapped my loins as she wriggled and writhed, crying out her enjoyment.

117

Above her jerking back I whispered, "Did you know what you were getting into when you left the *Athena*?"

Her head shook back and forth. "It was to be a holiday, with fun and games. You know? A little *besogne,* a bit of *paßer.*"

I could not carry on an extended conversation, not with sixteen *fentes* yet to be taken care of, but I had to know a few facts. I went on talking.

"Are you and your husband members of S.E.L.L.?"

"No, of course not. Just friends."

Her hips were getting ready to explode. I asked, "And the others? Fleur? Ilona Fortescu? Angelique?"

"O-only Georges! Aaaaagh!"

Her scream echoed in my ears as she jerked into her *comble du bonheur,* gasping and crying out. I felt hands catch my arms, yank me away.

I fell on my back on the next cot. A woman wearing black nylon stockings and a garterbelt flung herself on top of me. She squatted down in the posture known to the ancients as riding the Hectorean horse: knees apart, resting on stockinged feet on either side of my thighs.

"Thanks, sweetie," I murmured.

This was an easy position for me. The woman in the garterbelt, eyes wide open and glazed with delight, did all the work, driving herself with metronomic steadiness in a pounding beat. All I had to do was lie there.

I was grateful for the break. Servicing so many women is tiring to the muscles. My sexual muscle was still in great shape—in the *effect de la pendaison* of the French—but the rest of me was getting bushed fast. So I welcomed this break in pubic relations.

I even cheated a little. It felt so good just lying there I let the woman go on and on, spending more time with her than I had with any of the others. But the remaining fifteen caught on, and began a steady chant.

"Enough! Enough! Enough!"

"Yeah," I nodded. "And thanks again, honey."

The woman flopped on her cot and just lay there as I advanced upon Fleur Devot. The little blonde starlet was not as cocky as she had been aboard the *Athena*. She had lost some of her arrogance.

"I'm afraid," she whimpered as I yanked her off the bed and made her stand on her right foot while lifting her left leg.

"You jet-setters," I snorted as I invaded her *puits d'amour*.

She tried to speak but she could only gasp as I enjoyed her in the traditional *hari-vikrama-utthita-bandha* posture of the Hindu love experts. In a standing mirror to one side of the bed, I could watch the jiggle of her buttocks to my stabbings.

"But I didn't know——" she panted, between jiggles.

"Okay, okay. You on my side now?"

"*Mon Dieu! Oui! Oui!*"

She was shaking, rubbing her extraordinarily long nipples against my chest as her hands gripped my hips and her *hiatus divin* spasmed about my *herbe*. I held her almost tenderly. I mean, after all, bitch she might be, but I would rather have her on my side than against me.

Thinking about the Indian love postures was a big help. I began to go through them in my mind as Fleur Devot sank back onto the mattress of her cot, smiling blissfully as she stared at my *priapisme*.

"You're *trés magnifique*," she whispered.

The number eleven girl was pretty strong. She gave me a yank so I went staggering backward to land on my spine on her cot. She started to mount me in the St. George manner, but I turned her so her buttocks faced me as she straddled my loins. She rested her hands on my thighs and began to pump herself up and down and sideways, in that manner made famous by Rangoni and Ottavia in the Dialogues of a Courtesan.

I guess an erotologist like myself would figure I was in some sort of nirvanic nightmare. Here I was with two dozen assorted girls who could think of nothing but zigzag. I had the opportunity of a lifetime to study nationalistic reactions to certain caresses and to methods of copulation.

The trouble was, I couldn't see the forest for the trees.

119

There was just too much of a good thing. I could not retain my scholarly outlook; or at least, not all the time. I thought I was doing good to be able to lend each new *méfait* a touch of the unusual.

Right about now I began to worry.

Not about finishing my task. I figured I could make that all right. What bothered me was, what are these women going to want of me tomorrow? The next day? And the day after that? Nobody—not even King Roide!—can maintain such a pace. I needed an out—but fast.

I remembered the four girls—my lieutenants in the Amazon Army—who were waiting their own turns in the room outside this sororatorium. I shuddered in reaction, and the bare-bottomed beauty atop me screeched with delight as she thought she was causing it.

I stared at the bare buttocks shaking and jiggling like milky jello above my loins. Think, man! I told myself. There are twenty-eight lovelies on Thraxos waiting for you day and night. How did those sheiks do it, with their harems? Some of them had more than a hundred wives!

Egad!

Little miss pink-cheeks was all through, shaking and falling over my legs. I pushed her away and turned to the next cot.

Number twelve I took in the accepted *padm-asana* posture of the Hindus, sitting cross-legged on the floor, taking my brunette partner on my lap, with her hands on my shoulders. Number thirteen I pleasured lying on my side, lifting her left leg over my hip and sandwiching myself between those legs with my head propped up by my hand as my left arm was bent at the elbow. It is the perfect pose for a statue.

Fourteen, fifteen, sixteen and seventeen were variations on the *uttana-bandha* positions in which the woman lies prone with the man above. The whole secret in a lot of these love postures is the placing of the female legs. I put them upward and bent so the feet rested flat against my chest, or draped over my shoulders, or pushed back into the headboard of the bed, and under my armpits, while I was seated between their thighs.

Eighteen was an Egyptian girl, dusky of skin and with thick brown hair and big calf-eyes. She was lovely, and her breasts were very big for such a slim girl. Her lips seemed always to be apart, as if she found it difficult to breathe. I responded to her earthy lure, to the blue-tinted eyelids and long brown lashes, the tinted red fingernails, the hennaed soles of her feet.

She was serpentine in her movements, she slithered across her cot to me, her bee-stung lips lifted for my kiss. I kissed her lips, I stroked her heavy breasts, I pinched her nipples gently, and tugged on them. I could hear her moaning deep in her throat.

In ancient and in modern Egypt, its women have been renowned for their enjoyment of the mouth congress. My present companion was no exception. She let me drag her forward by her nipples until her mouth was on a level with my middle. With a low gasp she gripped me with her mouth.

I stood for her treatment until I felt that she had sufficiently stimulated herself. I drew her off the bed, made her do a handstand before me. Her slim, dusky thighs formed a fork. I stepped forward, drove downward, and heard her bleat with surprised pleasure. I locked my arms about her hips, half lifting her, and began the movements that brought shrill cries from her painted lips.

In rhythm to her cries, she brought into play a sidewise motion of her hips which Egyptian women call *ghunj*. These muscles permit the Egyptian woman to be an expert belly dancer. At the same time, by bringing into play the overdeveloped *constrictor cunni* muscles, she achieves a kind of sexual ecstasy known only to these sisters of the Nile.

She screeched and climaxed standing on her hands until her arms could hold her no longer. Then she dropped straight down and brought me with her, to end our delights groveling on the floor.

A hand pulled me up and toward a cot. A naked woman, with skin so dark she might have had mulatto blood in her veins, was grinning at me with a kind of erotic madness. Her I threw down upon the mattress on her back, and with

121

her the *el mokeurmeutt* of the Arab erotologists, with the legs of my companion straight upward so that the soles of her feet faced the ceiling. On the next cot I tried the *rekeud el air*, on my back with my knees drawn up to my chest while the Greek girl who was number twenty sat down upon me, braced with her back to the undersides of my thighs.

My next love-in lovely was an Albanian, I was sure, as I took her in the *el keurchi* manner, standing upright, belly to belly. She had long blonde hair that fell down to her plump buttocks, caressing the hands with which I gripped her rump as I aided her in the *neza'el dela* movements.

"Albania?" I breathed into her ear as her hips picked up the beat. She was gasping for breath, but her head nodded.

I thought about Albania and its ties with Red China as I fed delight to her soft white body. If Mao Tse-tung was interested in the mermen caper, this compound on the island of Thraxos must have feelers stretched across all the world. I could imagine Mao ordering a million of his fanatic followers to submit to the operations which would turn them into mermen. A striking force such as that, emerging from the ocean anywhere in the world, was a secret weapon terrible enough to turn even Uncle Sam and Ivan himself into worrywarts.

I slid from the Albanian into the arms of a lush Italian beauty. Her skin was brown with sunlight, her hair was long and dark. She was an eel slithering her nakedness against my own, sliding her heavy breasts across my chest and downward onto my belly, bending over and finally falling to her knees. Her hands held her fleshy globes, massaging me with them gently and for such a long time that the remaining two women began to cry out in something approaching impatience.

The Italian girl lifted her doe-eyes to me, gasping, head thrown back. I could see her swollen nipples gripped between her forefingers and thumbs and I realized that she was inducing her own pleasure just by that act. I waited, standing before her, until her breath came soft and moist, until she rubbed her face against my belly, clinging to my

122

thighs with both arms as she dragged her nipples up and down against my hard thighs.

Then she moaned and slumped.

I stepped toward the next to last cot. To my surprise, the little French maid Angelique was there, eyeing me as if I were some sort of god. She did not speak, except with her glowing eyes. She simply held out her arms to me.

I did not crash down on her as she apparently wanted. I caught her hip, I slipped her over on elbows and knees and took her in the manner of the ram, so that my hands could hold her dangling breasts while our loins worked the age-old rhythms of side to side and front and back. In a few short seconds she was wailing out her pleasure. I had forgotten for the moment that Angelique was but recently a non-virgin. The sights and sounds of what she had seen in this room must have been enough to set her off by herself, long before I reached her.

One woman remained: Ilona Fortescu.

"They made me go last," she told me with a frightened smile as I put a knee on her cot. "They consider me an enemy. After all, Georges was a good friend of Ernst Bachmann."

I fell forward on her soft, mature body. This woman I wanted to tease, to hurt. She had played the part of Judas goat with me, luring me unsuspectingly into that trap on the *Athena* deck. I owed her a lot of pain.

She must have seen something of this in my eyes, because she moaned and shook her head from side to side. "No, please! Don't blame me. Georges made me do it. It wasn't my fault."

"You could have warned me," I grunted.

She was trying to capture me with her thighs, opening and closing them, twisting and pivoting under me. From time to time she would press kisses on my jaw and throat and, when she could drag my head down with her bare arms fastened on my neck, to my lips. Ilona had begun to whimper.

I let her go on working herself up by what she was doing. Fear and her own bodily need for satisfaction ate in her

123

like white-hot flames. She was afraid of me; she knew I ought to cuff her about for the way she had tricked me on the *Athena*, but her flesh-wants were too great to be denied.

This soft, pampered woman was rousing those sadomasochistic instincts which lie deep under the veneer of every civilized male. I wanted vengeance. I would have my vengeance upon her. I caught her shapely white legs behind the knees, bending them far backward until her knees were pressed into her big breasts. Then I applied a sidewise pressure. She flipped over on her knees as if she had practiced the act.

Then when she was kneeling I caught her soft buttocks and lunged, driving myself forward into the *istaneh* position of the Arab erotogogists. Ilona Fortescu screamed, for she had become the *ghulamiyah*, the female used as a boy, she who submits her *ist* for the pleasure of the *el-istani*. The act was painful at first; the woman below me shrieked out the agony of her unfamiliarity with this mode of carnal congress.

Her agonized cries were music to my ears. Ilona Fortescu had given me to her husband and her guests to be lashed and tortured beyond endurance. She had looked on while one after the other these guests had teased me into a near madness. Now it was my turn to apply the branding iron to her psyche and to her *ist*. I thrust deeply, whispering my feelings to her ears.

"How does it feel, you bitch? Huh? Not so good, hey? Nobody's ever treated the great industrialist's wife to any indignity like this before, have they? See how you like being on the wrong end of the stick for a change!"

She was weeping now, sobbing in her pain.

To compensate her a little, since I am a tender-hearted fellow, I allowed myself the privilege of using the Japanese *mitokoro-zeme* technique employed at a time like this. I fondled her dangling breasts with my hands, I caught her clitoral bud and brought it into play.

Istaneh is popular in Persia, in the Arab world, and in certain parts of India. Along the coastal strip of North Afria, it is a complete way of sexual life. There are robber

124

bands in the remote regions of this eastern world called *luti*, who lie in wait for travelers and assault them in this manner. They flourished even in the days of the Prophet, who called down maledictions upon their heads.

In India, where Muslim women are quite zestful about this anal activity, they call it *gandhmari*. In China, it is 'back door blossom beating.' Nor were the ancient Greeks and Romans far behind their modern-day equivalents. Achilles often chose his friend Patroclus over his mistress, Briseus. Demophon enjoyed the beautiful hetira Nico, in such a way. Julius Ceasar was famed for his own anal addictions.

Ilona Fortescu was not suffering now. I had touched a masochistic nerve deep in her personality. Her wide white hips were squirming of their own volition. She was moaning not in pain but in rhapsodic delight. The play of my fingers at her nipples and clitoris had a lot to do with this pleasure. I was vaguely aware that Fleur Devot was standing beside the cot staring at us with wide, burning eyes, as her mouth hung open slackly. She seemed to be fascinated by the painful contortions of Ilona Fortescu's face.

Ilona had now begun a rhythmic quivering, a wriggling from head to hips that revealed how totally she had become involved in what was being done to her. I used her curving back for a support as I became the *abu hhimlat*, the daddy of all diddlers, as the Egyptians name the man who can go on and on in carnal copulation with a female.

The woman under me shook all over, groaning. Beside the cot, a sobbing Fleur Devot matched her, groan for groan, shaking all over in a masochistic trance.

"No more," I heard Ilona whimper. "Please! No more."

We fell apart. Ilona lay gasping and shaking on the bedsheets. I still knelt behind her, avoiding the hands that reached for me.

"Enough's enough, girls," I told them.

They did not believe me. They thrust their breasts against me, front and back, their hands reached down to grip and fondle, their lips poured words calculated to excite a dead man. I was not dead, not yet. But I might be if this went on much longer.

125

I pushed the hands aside. I made it to my feet. I dove like a fullback past hips that had cradled me and thighs that had wrapped their soft strength about various parts of my body. I thrust my way between these panting, whimpering women until I reached the door leading to the anteroom.

"Later, later, later," I kept saying.

If there was to be any later, I needed rest. I am a real *abu hhimlat* all right, thanks to my peculiar make-up, but I am still human. I opened the door and staggered through the doorway.

A man with a gun in his hand was facing me.

I did not need to ask who the man was. His ferocious grin, his sheer size—he towered all of six feet six inches and was broad in proportion to his height, all of it solid muscle—told me this must be Henri Vachon.

"Well, well," he murmured. "We have quite a man here, don't we? You must be this professor the girls have been telling me about."

My Amazon lieutenants were standing with their behinds to the far wall, their eyes bulging in fright and fascination as they looked from me to the huge Frenchman. They stopped looking at the Frenchman when they discovered that my priapism had in no way abated, despite my activity in the room with the two dozen women. Stella Marakza was crying softly to herself, probably visualizing me dead in another moment or two. I felt like crying myself.

The revolver in the hand of Henri Vachon did not waver.

"I intend to kill you," he muttered softly.

I shrugged, trying to be casual. "Anybody can pull a trigger," I told him. "It is the coward's way."

His eyelids flickered. I figured maybe I had touched a raw nerve. He was the biggest and probably the strongest man on the island. He was French, as well, and a corner of my mind told me the French are expert at *savate*.

For an instant, my fate hung on his pride.

"Coward?" he asked softly.

I spread my hands. "A brave man would try to stop me

126

with his bare hands. Not that he could do it."

Again the eyelids flickered, and I thought I could see raw pride deep inside his black eyes. He made a little motion with his gun toward the girls.

"They are your friends. If I let go the gun, they'll swarm all over me. I have no desire to be touched by—women."

He was a merman. The chemicals and the radiations that had altered the hormones of the other mermen would have affected him as well. He did not like women any more.

"There's a door behind me. Why not make them wait in there? You can lock them in with the others while you try to take me with your bare hands."

His grin was cruel. "I will break your back for you," he boasted. "I will do that after I have taken you *en l'inition postérieur!*"

I laughed at him. The pride in his eyes turned to hot rage, and there was a snarl in his throat as he gestured at the women with his gun.

"In the next room, you four! Hurry."

The girls looked at me. I nodded, saying, "Go on, girls. I'll finish this *con* off, and release you in a few moments."

Henri growled like a dog, staring at me.

The girls did what I asked. One by one they trooped past me, their sad eyes telling me they were sure they would never see me alive again. I patted the last one, Yusefa Suleyman, on her dusky behind as a little encouragement for her to hope.

Out of the corner of my eye I saw movement.

I crouched down. The big Frenchman was hurling himself at me feet first. I assume he fancied himself as a *savate* expert. Had those big boots landed, I would have been out of the fight right away. They would have driven me into the wall, knocking the breath out of me.

I crouched. My hands came up. I caught those boots, twisting them. Henri let out a yell as his head dropped to thump hard on the floor. I aimed a kick with my bare heel at the side of his jaw. My heel landed seconds after the back of his head hit the carpet.

A smaller man would have been out cold.

Henri Vachon did not lose his senses. He was staggered,

127

though, and he needed a moment to get his breath. I did not give him that precious time. In a fight to the finish like this, when neither man battles by any special rules, it was every man for himself with whatever method he could use to win.

Death waited for the loser.

So I landed with both bare feet and all my weight on his solar plexus. The breath whooshed out of his lungs. He gagged and suffered under me while I leaped off him and onto the floor. I dropped, bringing the edge of my right hand across his throat.

I can crack a two-inch plank with that karate blow.

I damn near broke his neck, but I missed the vital Adam's apple because he turned his head to one side. At the same time, his big hands tried for a strangle hold on my own throat. My body had been moving forward as my karate chop landed, so I was able to clobber the back of his neck with my knee. I went on over his prostrate body, landed on my palms and did a body flip to land on my bare feet.

I whirled. Henri Vachon was getting up.

My left fist traveled three feet and landed solidly on his nose. The big Frenchman bellowed and dove for me with his arms held straight forward, fingers spread wide. I reached out, I grabbed his right wrist.

I turned my back and yanked his right arm down across my shoulder in the approved technique for the *ippon seoi nage,* which breaks down in English to the shoulder throw. I gave the judo hold all I had, dropping unto a crouched position under his weight, and straightening at the same time that I yanked down on his arm.

The Frenchman rose upward into the air, head toward the floor. He seemed almost to hover there in mid-air before he came crashing down. I drove my bare foot into his face, the heel hitting his nose hard and breaking it at the exact moment of his impact.

Dirty fighting? You bet it was.

But I was fighting to stay alive. Henri Vachon was fighting to kill me—slowly, by bending my back across his knee until it cracked. We had no referee, no ropes around

128

our little arena. This was an elemental battle for life itself. You do anything you can at a time like that, against a man six feet six inches tall and maybe two hundred and sixty pounds in weight.

If you don't, you die.

The Frenchman lay breathing harshly on the floor for several seconds, while I got my own wind back. He was suffering; I could see that. His nose was bleeding, and pain was etched in furrows across his face and neck.

Then he moved his right hand.

I had forgotten he had thrust the revolver into his belt as he came for me. His right hand was burrowing under his body for it. He had had a bellyful of fighting with his bare hands. He was going to put a bullet in my belly, and the hell with anything like an even fight.

I took a running jump. One foot hit the back of his head, the other came down in the small of his back. His forehead hit the floor. His spine came damn near breaking. .

I whirled and dropped so I straddled his back. His right hand held the gun, and he was bringing it out from under him. I drove my left knee into the curve of his upper spine, and my right forearm about his neck, below his jaw. I grabbed my right wrist with my left hand and applied pressure.

His neck came back and back, bending at an awkward angle. At the same time, his right hand slithered past his rib cage until I could see the barrel of his gun. I squeezed harder with my forearm.

His neck was close to snapping.

The sound of his breathing was like a foot dragging out of wet mud, moist and soggy. My right forearm was all but shutting off his supply of air.

The gun came out into the open. It turned toward me. I was going to be a dead man in another second.

CHAPTER EIGHT

I dared not release my hold to go for the gun. Henri Vachon would have flipped me off his back with one huge heave of his massive body. It was all I could do to drag his head backwards, using every last iota of my strength, while watching that gun barrel turn to stare into my face.

The hand that held the gun was quivering. The gun barrel shook back and forth. The Frenchman had had to turn his hand around so he could shoot behind him. It was an unnatural pose but it was all he could do under the circumstances.

I held my breath.

The muscles in my arms bulged.

kraaaaaaakkk

I slumped forward, letting out my breath. I had broken his neck. I felt his body shudder under me, saw his arm fall, watched and heard the thump as the revolver hit the carpet and skidded away.

Henri Vachon died, body jerking, breath whistling in his throat. I lay across him, my heart pounding savagely in relief, my muscles turned to water in the reaction to my near-death. I waited until I was breathing more or less normally before I got up and staggered toward the door.

When my Amazons saw me framed between the jambs, they let out wild screeches of delight and leaped for me. I went down under their combined assaults.

Fortunately they realized my exhaustion. Eager hands raised me to my feet. Soft lips and soft voices cooed to me, assuring me I would be well taken care of. One girl even found time to congratulate me on my victory over the big

130

Frenchman, telling me that I was now the unquestioned ruler of the island of Thraxos.

"Put me to bed, honey," I told the redheaded Janine.

They supported me between them, out of the anteroom and up a narrow flight of stairs to an upstairs bedroom. Soft hands pushed me down between the sheets and drew blankets and bedspread over me. Gentle lips kissed me to sleep.

I did not dream. I just lay like a dead man.

When I woke, morning sunlight was streaming into the room. Some thoughtful chick must have tiptoed in with my clothes, because a shirt and slacks, shoes and socks lay across a nearby chair with a black leather gunbelt and holster that held a Luger automatic.

I got dressed and went downstairs.

My stomach rumbled, informing me that I had neglected it shamefully. As I stepped out into the sunshine I found Fleur Devot waiting for me.

"I am your personal bodyguard, your majesty," she told me with a dimpled smile. She was pertly pretty in a drill jacket and mini-skirt, a sort of unofficial uniform, I assumed, for my Amazon army. Her right hip held a holstered revolver.

"Can you use that thing?" I asked.

She shrugged with Gallic fatalism. "Of course not. But I am the only one who really knows that. It would take a very brave man to try and find out, *n'est ce pas*?"

It would. I let her take me to the dining area. With Fleur waiting on me personally, I finished off a pint of tomato juice, a half-dozen scrambled eggs and a half pound of bacon. Plus three cups of steaming coffee.

When I was done, I asked, "What now?"

"There are to be executions," she smiled.

"Oh? Whose?"

"The men and the women who refuse to join us. Men like Georges Fortescu and those among the mermen who do not admit you are our king. As for the women—well, that blonde dancer Donna Romminet and her friend Barbe are among them, with a couple of others."

I felt this was kind of high-handed treatment, but when

131

you fight S.E.L.L., you fight the way I had battled Henri Vachon—all out and with no quarter given. We had offered the boys and girls a choice. They had chosen not to join us.

"How will they die?"

Fleur frowned. "I am not sure. Janine said something about *ontos*—Greek for a 'thing'. It will do the killing for us, I understand. There is a place among the crags on the western tip of the island, not far from here, that forms a kind of hole in the rocks, partially filled with water. They will be cast into that hole."

Like sacrifices to Poseidon in the olden days. Man does not change much over the centuries. As victims have been thrown from clifftops before, so would they be hurled again. Sappho had given her life in this manner, say the old myths.

I went with Fleur to the anteroom that was our headquarters. Janine Karthos and Theophano Linitka were waiting for me. Stella was out drilling the girl soldiers, with Yusefa attending to the details of the executions.

"We're going to have to do something about these girls," I told the redhead. "Fun's fun and all that, but I can't go on servicing them the way I did yesterday."

"You're our king," protested Throphano.

"Better a live king than a dead one," I pointed out. "Besides, I have an idea as to how we can make everybody happy."

"How's that?" asked Janine, sitting up straight.

"Tell you later. First things first. I understand we're getting rid of the dissenters in our group?"

"Oh, the executions. Yes, they're scheduled for half an hour from now. I suppose we might as well get moving."

I walked between Janine and Theophano, with Fleur a step to my rear. I noticed that she walked with a hand on her gunbutt, as if she were expecting an attack on me at any moment. I did not know whether to find her attitude reassuring or alarming. It was nice to have her at the ready in case of trouble, but what kind of trouble did she expect to happen?

Some white object glinting in the Aegean sunlight caught

132

my eyes. I slowed my pace and changed direction, walking toward it. From this distance, it seemed to be an upright marble slab.

Fleur came flouncing at my heels. "What is it?" I asked her.

"I don't know, your majesty."

We came to a stop a few feet away, and I understood. This was a recent grave, the markings where sod had been laid on top of it clear to read. The gravestone was blank. I walked to the other side. There were no letters on the reverse side either.

A body laid to rest. Name unknown. But why was there no name? My curiosity was roused, scratching at my brain. I made a mental note to ask Ernst Bachmann about this later.

We walked back to join the others.

Stella had lined the women up in rows. They burst into cheers at sight of me, remembering my great moment with all twenty-four of them yesterday. I grinned and saluted them as I stepped out to lead them toward the hole in the crags where the *ontos* dwelled.

"What is the *ontos*?" I asked Theophano.

"Nobody knows, lord. I think that at one time many, many centuries ago there was a temple here, where the compound now stands. A temple to Poseidon, I believe it was. Men captured in battle were flung to the *ontos* that lived in the hole. It must still live there. Ernst Bachmann has dropped a few men into its lair to teach any rebels to obey the rules."

"Hmmm. A shark, maybe. Or an octopus?"

Yusefa, with half a dozen of the women soldiers, was already at the flat stretch of rock that formed a collar about the hole. Studying the rock, I noticed marks that indicated the collar had not always been flat. Hammers and chisels had worked here to make it into a broad platform.

Many mermen, Eduardo Herrara and his mistress, Juana Batione, Alain Maillot and Georges Fortescu were among those standing here with their wrists tied behind them. I saw the blonde dancer and her girl friend among

133

the few women who had chosen to be executed rather than join my Amazons. Barbe Serrelle looked as if she had been crying.

"Must they die?" I asked Janine.

"They must, your majesty. We just don't have the manpower to keep them all as prisoners under guard. And we don't dare trust them to set free."

The mermen I had no pity for. They were S.E.L.L. agents, as was Geroges Fortescu and, quite probably, Eduardo Herrara and Alain Maillot. It was only the women that touched my heart. Then I reflected that a lot of them might be S.E.L.L., too—especially Juana Batione and Donna Romminet.

"The women first," snapped Yusefa.

A hand pushed at Donna. She took a step forward, her legs acting rubbery. She was close to fainting. Barbe came to stand beside her. As one, they stepped off the stone collar and dropped like stones past the jagged edges of the ancient rocks. They hit the water in the pit, making a big splash.

I held my breath, peering down.

They sank out of sight. Then through the clear, translucent waters, they kicked their way upward to the surface. Barbe was screaming in stark terror by this time. Her nerve was completely gone. Others were being thrust over the rim and toward that dark, deadly hole in the rocks that was filled with cold ocean water.

Overhead, the Aegean sun could have been the same that looked down upon the sacrifices to Poseidon that took place here more than three thousand years ago. In the days when Trojan Hector was fighting on the plains of Troy, the priests of the sea god were thrusting captives over this same rim of rock. The same warmth that beat on them, now touched all of us.

I stared as if hypnotized down into that rocky opening. The gray stone of its walls was jagged, rough. One merman tore open a long gash in his thigh when he fell against one such razor-sharp rock thrust. When he hit the water, the red blood flowed out to mingle with the deep blue water.

The last merman went over. Close to twenty men and

women were down there, kicking with their feet, hands tied behind them, trying to keep their heads above water. The hole was possibly fifty feet across, and the water there was very deep. There was plenty of room for all of them.

And for something else.

I heard Donna Romminet scream as she lifted her face to the sun and stared with blind horror, upward at the collar where we were standing. The scream ended in a gurgle as her body was drawn downward. Her open, screeching mouth gurgled as it filled with water. Then she was gone.

Now the water boiled around the others as pallid white bodies jostled and thumped about the men and women. I gasped and felt nausea churn up inside my middle. Those were sharks down there—albino sharks! Their bodies were a fishbelly white, their eyes were pink. Their mouths gaped, displaying rows of sharp teeth that clamped on legs and arms and hips.

Madness erupted in that death hole.

Men and women fought with nails and teeth as they tried to battle the ravenous sharks that fed upon their flesh. I do not think those voracious killers of the deep lived in the ocean; I think they came from some subterranean sea where there is darkness and very little light from one end of the year to the other. Long ago the priests of Poseidon learned of their existence and fed them to keep them coming back to this hole that looked from their dark world into ours.

The smell of blood carries far in the water to the senses of a shark. They had learned over the centuries to expect food—living food—to be waiting for them when they came to eat. The priests had kept their bellies full. So had the mermen. Now it was the turn of some of those mermen to die here as they had made others die.

Blood bubbled into the churning waters.

One by one, by bits and pieces, the sacrifices were torn apart by those hungry sharks. The shark is not a common occupant of the Mediterranean, except for the whale shark. These were killer sharks, deadly and vicious denizens of some unknown sea below the island. Today they were being fed as never before.

135

I put out a hand. I found I was holding Fleur. "Let's get out of here," I told her. "I can't stand much more of this."

To my surprise, Fleur wanted to go on staring down into that hellhole of horror. She was holding her breath in excitement, and her eyes blazed with something like lust. I remembered the Colosseum, where Roman matrons had found themselves stirred to a fleshly furore by the blood spilled on the arena sands in the days when the Caesars ruled the world.

My Amazons were sisters under the skin to those Roman matrons. Right now I was the only male in this laboratory compound. My girl soldiers would be expecting me to take care of them. Include little blonde Fleur in that group too. She was pressing her behind against me, turning her blue eyes up, begging with them.

"Do me, please—the way you did Ilona!"

I grinned down at her. This was the nymphet who had teased me with the lollipop, the nymphet I had raped on the *Athena.* I remembered how the pain in her loins had triggered off the lust that accepted me as her sex partner after I had hurt her sufficiently.

I put a hand under her short military jacket and fondled her soft buttocks. She had on black nylon panties under her jacket. She quivered to my caresses.

Nobody was looking at us, everybody was staring down into the shark hole. I pinched her behind hard. Fleur moaned, and her eyes rolled back in her head as she sagged against me.

I remembered her bitchiness, her arrogance. But I began to reevaluate those traits. Maybe she was so obnoxious because she wanted to get a spanking, to get slammed around. Masochists are like that. They'll do damn near anything to rouse a person to savage anger so this anger will be turned against them in punishment. The lollipop act was just one more manifestation of this submissive instinct. She had wanted me to break loose; she had wanted me to ravish her flesh.

There was something about her very willingness to be

136

punished and hurt that jabbed a corresponding cruelty in my male hormones. Here on Thraxos the masks were coming off. Fleur was no longer a pretty French starlet; she was a yielding female who needed pain to stimulate her.

I pinched again and she moaned.

"I have things to do," I told her cruelly. "Important things, Fleur. You have to wait. You aren't important enough for me to put those aside just to pleasure your body. You understand that, don't you?"

"Oh, yes, your majesty! I do understand. I'm not worthy of your attention. But I'll try to be."

I let her go with a slap on her soft rump.

"Janine," I called.

The redhead turned dreaming eyes at me. I told myself I still owed Janine, Stella, Theophano and Yusefa a go-go gambit between the sheets. They had to wait. I wanted to get the action started on this little island.

"I'm going to visit the mermen. I'll take Fleur along for protection. I intend to offer them a place with us—if they'll agree to join forces."

Janine scowled "They're no good to us."

"Yes, they are—as pirates."

She did not understand, but she was willing to go along with me. She nodded when I explained that with the mermen siding us, we could send them out to loot and steal by boarding ships and by raiding towns, much in the manner of the Barbary Corsairs more than two centuries ago.

Meanwhile, she would keep the Amazons busy.

The mermen presented no problem. With Fleur at my side, I invaded their little cubicles, I made them my proposition. These mermen had elected to join us to save their lives. What I offered was something each of them already had in his mind to do, for S.E.L.L.

"Instead of raiding ships for their scientific apparatus, or dragging off high-ranking officials to a S.E.L.L. prison —you'll steal gold and jewels."

I told myself, the end justifies the means. By turning this laboratory compound into a pirate lair, I would bring the navies of Greece and Turkey (united for a change), maybe even those of Italy and France, down upon our little Thrax-os haven. In the holocaust which would result, I'd be able to make a break for it.

The mermen were eager. This very night, they'd take their submarine out and go hunting for palatial yachts like the *Athena* or for small cruise ships ploughing the waters of the Aegean and Ionian Seas. I assured them every mer-man would get a share of the booty he brought back. The mermen would come back; I did not fear desertion, men such as they had become would find the facilities they needed only in this laboratory-compound.

They had heard how I killed Henri Vachon with my bare hands. I saw grudging respect and a faint fear in all their eyes. Their chemical-and-radiation-changed personalities compelled them to bow to a superior personality.

My next port of call was Ernst Bachmann.

He blustered at first when I entered his luxurious quarters. He was indignant at this treatment until I told him how the albino sharks had been fed. Then fright made livid furrows on his face, and he could not control the shaking of his hands.

"Wh-what do you want with me?"

"A little information, that's all. You can go on living here if you join forces with us. You can even go on—experimenting."

I wagged a finger at Fleur, standing beside me with her hand on the gun at her hip. "Beat it," I told her.

Obediently she went out and closed the door.

"The grave outside. Whose is it?"

"A woman lies buried there," he muttered.

I had been thinking hard about that grave, so I hazarded a guess. "You treated her with the same chemicals and radiation that altered men into mermen, didn't you?"

He nodded. I went on talking. "You didn't realize your radiations would affect the hormones of the men, changing them into homosexuals. What was the result on the woman?"

"She became nymphomaniacal. Hysterical with her need for sex. She all but attacked and raped every man in the compound. We had to—destroy her."

138

"I want you to treat every woman to that same radiation. Turn them into mermaids."

His surprise was laughable. "Are you mad? They'd attack us—you and me, as being the only males potent enough to satisfy their demands."

"No. I have a better use for them. Now, do as I say."

His smile was sly. "I'll need my notebooks. You took them."

"I'll put them at your disposal at every operation. I'll be standing by, to make sure you don't destroy them."

"I'm no martyr," he muttered. I believed him.

I went out, closing and locking the door behind me.

Everything was going according to the plan I had worked out. All that remained was to select the women to be turned into mermaids. I decided I would work this out with my four lieutenants.

None of the four raised any objections when I proposed my plan. Naturally I did not tell them what the effect of the operation would be; time enough for them to learn that after the event. I explained that we needed women who would go along with the mermen as officers, to direct the piracy, to make certain the mermen did not desert or take more than their share of the loot.

We agreed to put it to a vote of the women themselves. I did not anticipate any difficulty. When the amazons learned they would be getting their share of jewels and money, they would give my suggestion an unanimous vote of approval.

To keep so many women in a subservient mood, S.E.L.L. had been forced to dope them. It explained why these females had never revolted until yesterday. Bachmann had run out of the chemical he fed them, as prisons feed saltpeter to male prisoners, and Georges Fortescu had been ordered to fetch more.

The kegs that held these chemicals had been taken from the *Athena*. They reposed now in the laboratory storeroom. I did not need them; I wanted women whose senses were alert to do my bidding. But enough of the residue of the dope still remained in their systems to destroy their moral fibers.

The girls were ready for rape or robbery, believe me.

139

That very night, I was going to send out my first detachment of mermen. I needed some women to go with them. Every hand in the audience room was raised to volunteer. I selected ten, and Yusefa marched them across the compound walk to the operating room.

I sent Theophano to fetch Ernst Bachmann.

With Fleur at my side, I would be a witness to what happened. I was anxious to watch the technique so I could report back to Walrus-moustache about it. I went to Ernst Bachmann's office safe, took out his notebooks, and slipped them into an attaché case.

Bachmann was very proficient. His hands were deft as he filled his hypodermic cartridges and laid them out on an instrument table. One of the mermen was to serve as a nurse. There was an operating table set beneath a row of lenses in a shallow steel box fitted with a dozen cables. I gathered that this was the radiation machine which, in conjunction with the chemicals—or sea-serum—injected into their veins, would transfer a man into a creature able to live beneath the sea.

A woman came in, naked under a loose hospital gown.

The woman climbed on the table, the smock was opened and its flaps dropped downward so her body was revealed to the boxed lenses a yard above the table. I studied her body with a cool eye. I had made love to that body last night. I had entertained it with the wheelbarrow position.

As if she remembered this, her eyes sought mine. She smiled, winked. I smiled back at her and blew her a kiss. Then Ernst Bachmann took over. With cotton dipped in disinfectant, he cleaned an area on her upper left arm, then on her groin, then on her left thigh. He reached for a needle.

Three injections of the sea-serum. The woman winced each time, but with correspondingly less emphasis. Noting my interest, Bachmann smiled.

"The sea-serum puts them to sleep. They are asleep during the two hours they are under the radiation lenses."

He covered her closed eyes with little plastic cups. As she slept, she would remain utterly motionless, Bachmann assured me.

140

There would be a two-hour wait, and after that she would be kept asleep another two hours in sea water, under drugs. It was one of these mermen, so drugged, that the baroness had inadvertently walked in on, when she had been on Thraxos.

I was curious. I asked, "As we were driven here, we passed through a town, and several farmsteads. Haven't those people ever wondered what you might be doing here?"

Bachmann smiled, "We made cash contributions to the towns. We explained that we were experimenting with radiations, and that nobody would be hurt if they stayed clear of our compound. So far, nobody has been curious enough to find out what it is the radiation does."

I could spend no more time in the operations room.

Other matters demanded my attention.

The target for tonight was a small yacht owned by a rich Italian manufacturer. Luckily, S.E.L.L. keeps a file on such things; theirs is a far-flung operation—this laboratory-compound on Thraxos was only a small part of their setup—and they never knew when they might need to kidnap a person off the high seas or steal a bundle of cash from some yacht safe.

I marked the *Julia Ceasar* down for attack.

The submarine which would carry the mermen out into the Aegean lay at anchor in a hidden cove surrounded by high crags. I visited it with Fleur and Janine, explaining to Janine that a complement of ten mermen ought to be enough to board and take the yacht. With the mermen, I wanted a complement of twenty Amazons, to make sure the mermen did not rebel.

Janine nodded, "I'd like to volunteer for that duty."

At dusk, I went down to the little quay where the submarine was anchored and watched my troops march off to pirate the *Julia Caesar*. They were all armed, mermen and Amazons.

Fleur was nudging my elbow with her left breast as the submarine sank beneath the surface of the sea. I guess she figured it was time for me to pay her some attention. She made an appetizing sight in her military jacket and long

141

bare legs, I must admit. Knowing that only a pair of black nylon panties were under that jacket, aside from her own nakedness, was an added temptation.

But first I owed a visit to Yusefa, Stella and Theophano.

I had balled Fleur Devot last night in the dormitory. I had not so much as raised a finger to my lieutenants.

As I grinned down at Fleur, I said, "Tell Yusefa, Stella and Theophano to report to me in my rooms at nine sharp. Oh, yes—I want you there too, Fleur."

She smiled in utter delight and ran off to spread the word, heedless of the fact that the back flap of her military jacket went up and down to furnish delightful glimpses of her buttocks scarcely contained by the black nylon.

Poor Fleur! She was in for a bad night.

I had taken over the suite that had been assigned to the Fortescus. It boasted a large living room, an equally large bedroom with attached bath that looked a little like something out of a Roman bathing scene, with solid gold fixtures, king-sized tub and other assorted decorations and utilities. I mixed up a batch of martinis, switched on the stereo, and changed into a maroon lounging robe that fit me rather well, as the bathroom mirror attested. Georges Fortescu and I, before the albino sharks got him, had been something of the same size.

The girls were there right on time.

Stella was wearing a clinging evening gown of transparent silk under which an onlooker could catch glimpses of dark red nipples and a blonde pubic thatch. I on-looked liked crazy as she strolled in, breasts doing their provocative little bounce, hips swaying roguishly.

I tore my eyes away to stare at Yusefa Suleyman, who was wrapped in a long evening cloak of black satin. She started to drop it as her left foot—in a golden sandal—stepped over the threshold of my suite. As it fell, it revealed the fact that my Turkish bellydancer wore only a girdle of golden links and a gold satin panel about her plump hips. She had tinted her nipples a bright red and her eyelids a faint green. Her long black hair fell down her back to her solid buttocks. She was a walking invitation to venery.

142

Theophano Linitka wore a black lace jump suit, out of two holes in which her heavy white breasts protruded, shaking to her step. Between her navel and her upper thighs, only two black lace panels hid her sides. In front and back, the black lace left her naked from thighs to bellybutton.

I heard Fleur whimper. The little French starlet had planted her spine up against the wall and she was looking from each of the three girls to me, and back again. In her military jacket, she must have thought herself awfully dowdy alongside these glamazons.

She knew what was about to happen.

Theophano came toward me and plastered her soft white body and its black lace decoration right up against me. I was naked under the lounging robe. As her arms went about my neck and her pelvis brushed against mine, my manhood reacted with instant interest. She cooed as she rubbed it, as her soft red mouth opened for my kiss. I put my arms about her and began to stroke her soft, quivering buttocks. I lost myself in that tongue-darting kiss, that movement of female flesh against my own.

I felt pressure against my knuckles.

My eyes opened and I looked past Theophano's bare shoulder into Yusefa's smiling face. She was nudging herself against the backs of my hands that gripped the Greek girl's soft behind.

"Is this going to be a crowd thing?" I asked the soft lips that were caressing my own very wetly. Theophano nodded.

"We've talked it all over. We've decided."

"Oh? And what of me?"

Stella had come up behind me to press her breasts to my back and her *mons veneris* to my bottom. Her hands were sliding under the lounging jacket, up and down my naked chest and belly. Into my ear she crooned, "You are a king on the island, but in your own bedroom, you shall be our slave."

Yusefa was working herself to a froth against my knuckles. She panted, "You took two dozen women last night. Tonight you only have to take three."

"Eight times each," gurgled the Grecian lovely.

Fleur made a sound deep in her throat from where she was pressed against the wall. I turned my head and looked at her. She was going to get her full of masochistic pleasure.

"You stand guard, Fleur," I rasped. "Don't let anybody in."

"Except our plaything," laughed Stella.

Fleur gasped, "What about me?"

"Guess you'll just have to suffer, honey."

Blonde Stella was tugging at my lounging robe, sliding it down off my back, leaving me stark naked against the cooing, writhing Theophano. As my robe dropped, Stella replaced it with her soft palms, sliding them across my taut buttocks, up over my tensed, muscular back, and around under my arms to my sides.

I shook like a leaf in a windstorm.

Those hands on my back, red fingernails scratching, the gurgling Greek girl in front, caressing my straining manhood with her soft bare thighs, and Yusefa, in front of me and behind Theophano, arching her mons veneris against my knuckles. Three lush, fleshy women, all working on my lone male body, slowly and with feeling.

I was ready to blow up.

Off to one side, Fleur was sobbing softly.

It was almost as hard on her as it was on me.

144

CHAPTER NINE

Yusefa was drawing back and away from me, arms over her head to display her shaven armpits. The stereo was grinding out appropriate music for a Turkish belly dance, and Yusefa was going to oblige me.

I stared at her revolving belly and shimmying thighs with my eyes while Theophano was kissing my throat and Stella was reaching down past my middle to grope at my loins for what she wanted to hold. Sandwiched between two women who were as good as naked, watching a third woman who showed even more of her body to my bulging eyes, I felt like a sex-crazed sultan.

Maybe the girls figured that after last night, I needed some foreplay before they ganged up on me. Whether I did or not, I was sure getting it. And liking every lascivious moment of it.

Yusefa was holding her arms out at right angles to her body. Her tinted eyelashes were fluttering as she watched Theophano sinking downward, as Stella was scratching my most sensitive sense with her long red fingernails. Her lush red mouth was open to aid her breathing as she widened her thighs, crouching down, and sent her olive-tinted belly bobbling like a beach ball spinning.

I was panting just as hard as the Turkish girl.

Theophano was kneeling and drawing her breasts back and forth across my erotic excitement. Behind me, Stella was kissing me all the way down to my rump. I quivered and shook between those stroking breasts and those kissing lips. I felt as if every muscle in my body were standing up and going rigid.

145

I looked as Yusefa went into a grind and bump. The gold satin panel, modeled on the stripper's panel of the good old U.S.A., was beginning to lift and flap in front of her pelvis. Her bold black eyes dared me not to be affected by what I was seeing. I could not take her dare. I was too affected already, because every time her satin panel went flying, it showed more and more of what the real Yusefa Suleyman was like. I saw her inner thighs; I saw the soft flesh jiggle; I saw the dark forest of her groin. All the while her black eyes blazed a challenge at me to which my male flesh was responding like a pointer on the scent of a pheasant.

The belly dance—the *res es-surreh* of the Arabs—is as old as our recorded history. Slave girls danced it before the Pharaohs of Egypt, they entertained such notables of the ancient world as Hammurabi of Babylon and Sennacherib of Assyria with their ventral contortions. Bits of pottery and Egyptian friezes show them in their gyrations. In Roman times, the women of Gades were especially noted for their exciting performances, so much so that a Gadean dance has come to mean the same as our more modern *danse du ventre*.

In 1890, a woman known as Little Egypt introduced a watered-down version of the bellyroll to United States audiences at the Chicago World Fair. There is a world-famed group of such dancers, the Ghawazi. A branch of this group—the Ouled Nails of Northern Africa—flourishes from Casablanca to Cairo.

The Turks are a part of the belly dance tradition, I reminded myself as I watched Yusefa contort her soft, olive-tinted flesh before my bulging eyes. Her tantalizing twists were being helped along by the ministrations of the girls who knelt before and behind me. I was making a kind of gurgling sound in my throat that was the preliminary to a pounce on one or maybe even all three of my tormentors.

I was swaying back and forth.

Stella grabbed my waist and yanked me backwards. Theophano screeched and leaped, sinking herself down on my most upstanding attraction. Yusefa came toward us, belly bobbing and thighs jerking. She laughed down at my

146

contorted face—Theophano was doing a bump and grind on my puffed-up pride, accounting for the faces of agonized joy I was making—and then came to stand over my head.

I stared up at the Turkish delight Yusefa was showing me. My back was cradled on the soft feminine body of Stella Marakza while the Greek glamor girl slowly did the split above me, bringing her halvah down so I could sample its delicate flavor.

I sampled it while Yusefa squealed and wriggled.

Somebody was sobbing off to one side. Dazedly I realized it must be Fleur, watching us with wide eyes and writhing in her personal torment. If she was a masochist, she sure was getting her bang-bangs, being unable to participate in what she was seeing. I felt a little sorry for her.

However, to be honest about it, I had very little feelings left over for Fleur. My trio of temptresses was taking care of my feelings. Theophano leaped and bobbed, Yusefa squirmed and panted, while Stella was getting her kicks by being squashed beneath me, moving her hips in a steady twisting, back and forth against my buttocks, so that I could feel the spur of her distended clitoral bud.

At a signal, the girls played switch.

Yusefa moved forward, Stella squirmed out from under, Theophano lay down beside me. As my Turkish dancer engulfed me, I engulfed Stella crouched over my face, while the Greek girl caressed Yusefa and me with her long red fingernails.

Our sexual saraband went on and on.

After half an hour the girls switched again. And then again, thirty minutes later. And so on, *ad infinitum,* all through the rest of the night.

Theophano was the first girl to fall asleep, Stella was next, and then the belly dancer. They were snoring in minutes. It was now that Fleur left her post by the door and crawled on her hands and knees across the carpet to me.

"Please," she whimpered. "Please! Take me, take me."

I pushed her away, saying, "I had to ball these babes, honey. I have to keep them loyal to me the only way I

147

know how. Besides, I'm tired. Haven't you been watching what I've been doing?"

"Yes! Oh, yes—I have. That's why——"

"Some other time," I grumbled.

I turned over on my front and lay there, starting to fall asleep. Fleur crawled to me, placed herself on top of me, and began kissing my neck. It did her no good; I was already dreaming.

I woke to the touch of a hand on my shoulder.

"The submarine has returned, your majesty," a soft voice told me. "It's docking now at the marina."

I opened my eyes to the sight of Fleur's taut white face. There were faint purple rings under her eyes and her blonde hair was all disheveled, falling about her shoulders like a wheaten mop. Her red mouth was quivering.

"Good," I muttered. "Fetch my clothes."

She stood while I got dressed, staring hungrily at my every move. I said guiltily, "We have to get the show on the road, honey. We have no time for bedwork, right?" She nodded, on the verge of tears.

I felt like a heel. It would have taken only fifteen or twenty minutes to give her what she needed. Well, if she liked to suffer, and it had become quite evident to me that she did, she was getting a bellyful of it.

We marched out into the sunlight and down to the marina. Fleur walked with her head held high, she would have died rather than let the other women see what she was suffering.

The women were leaving the submarine, saluting me, satified looks on their faces. My redheaded lieutenant came to meet me, smiling happily.

"A good haul, your majesty. Half a million dollars in cold cash and probably a million more in jewels. Valued in American money, that is, though it's in Italian lire. How've things been going here?"

"Just fine," I told her, seeing her green eyes stab at Fleur and with the sure instincts of a woman in such matters read her face all too well. She said nothing, just made a moué with her pouty lips.

148

She hooked her arm in mine. "I'll give my report in private, if you like," she told me.

"Come along, Fleur," I murmured, as to a dog at heel.

In my office, Janine Karthos explained how the submarine had ejected its mermen through the escape hatch while submerged thirty feet below and fifty yards behind the pleasure yacht *Julia Caesar*. When they were on their way, swimming just below the surface, she brought the submarine up to periscope depth to watch what went on.

She had seen them climb the side of the yacht, using sucker-discs on their hands and knees. She had seen nothing then, until a light blinked on and off at the yacht's stern, which was the mermen's signal for mission accomplished.

"They told me all about it when they returned, of course," she nodded. "It was a lead-pipe cinch. There hasn't been any piracy in these waters since the American war with the Barbary corsairs more than a century and a half ago. The women screamed and fainted, and the men handed over their money without a fight. The mermen were on the yacht for less than thirty minutes."

"A good beginning," I complimented her.

It was only a beginning, however.

In the next few days I alternated my time between the operation room where Ernst Bachmann was turning many of the women into mermaids, and the beds of these sea-girls where I tried to satisfy their intensified lusts.

Frankly I was getting pretty tired of playing the part of human studhorse. The fun was gone out of it. It had become a chore. Not only that, but those hungry pussycats were wearing me out. I ate handfuls of vitamin tablets; I made Ernst Bachmann inject me with syringes of vitamin E, the fertility vitamin; I dined on oysters at every meal.

Fleur tagged after me with her blue eyes begging for a few minutes of my bed time. I had none left over for her. Even Janine I had to bypass, because the mermaids were getting so out of hand with their sex needs I was needed to keep them under some sort of control.

When Ernst Bachmann had made twenty mermaids, I

149

called a halt. I summoned my lieutenants to a conference. I laid down the law.

"I need help," I told them honestly. "These nymphs will kill me if I don't get it."

"I'll die if I don't get it too," muttered the redhead darkly. She had been getting as bad as Fleur, dogging my steps and hinting broadly that she needed to be laid.

"I have an idea," I said. "We need sturdy young men to take my place. Let's go out and get them."

Yusefa squealed and clapped her hands. Theophano nodded happily. Janine merely muttered that she needed more than just one man by this time. Fleur stared at me hopefully. I guess she was figuring that if my bed duties were cut down, she might get to hold me in her arms.

I called a meeting of the mermaids, informing them of our plan. They howled their approval. No matter what they thought of me, they figured there just wasn't enough of me to go around.

We would pick a select group of mermen and mermaids. I would go along with the raiding party, ostensibly to lead the party but privately—a fact which I did not share with anyone—to make my escape, if I could.

If I made my escape with the notebooks I kept always within reach of my hand, I would reveal the location of the pirates' lair to the police of Istanbul and Athens, so the united Greek and Turkish air force might bomb the laboratory compound out of existence.

"Where'll we raid?" wondered Yusefa. "Not Turkey! I would feel like a traitor."

"And not Greece or its islands," hastily added Theophano.

"Italy's too far," murmured Janine.

"How about Albania?" I offered.

We got out maps and checked on Albania, which bordered on the Greek state of Arcas. There was a small fishing village, Vlanditsa, across from the Greek island of Corfu, which looked promising. Albanians feast on oysters, mussels and fish which they drag from the Adriatic Sea. Vlanditsa was a sleepy place, Theophano assured me, with no more than one policeman. It would be ripe for attack from the waters that fed its inhabitants.

We would leave at dawn, and arrive the following day at nightfall. In the dark, the mermen and the mermaids would make their raid. Janine looked at me with bed-bounce in her eyes but I smiled and shook my head.

For the first night in a long time I slept unaccompanied and unmated. The sun would rise early tomorrow. I meant to be energetic and enthusiastic when it did.

I took Fleur with me as I walked down the stone path to the marina after breakfast. I do not think I could have left her behind, except by locking her in a room. She was armed to her pretty white teeth with an automatic rifle and a small Belgian automatic, holstered on her hip.

Only the mermen knew how to run the submarine. The mermaids, Janine, Fleur and I were along for the ride. The *Triton* had been a Nazi U-boat in the last world war, with twin diesel motors capable of generating close to three thousand horsepower, so its speed reached a top figure of eighteen knots.

I was not too well acquainted with a submarine and welcomed this chance to learn something of its functions. My first discovery was that the interior of a 1940 German submersible was more cramped than an American undersea craft. Every inch of space is accounted for, and from its forward port hydroplane to its twin rudders it was over two hundred and twenty-odd feet in length.

The motors throbbed as the propellors carried us along the surface until the gongs clanged with the rig for diving alert. The hatch was secured, even while the klaxon was whooping, while the below-decks men twirled and pulled levers.

"All secure," a merman shouted.

"Take her down," came the order.

We sank into a sea over which Ulysses had sailed his ship on his long voyage from Troy. The submarine moved quietly, just humming to its motor throbbings. You did not experience the sensation of being underwater. There was just the faint, forward surge underfoot and the awareness of motor noises in your ears.

It grew boring, standing in the control room where the

steel shaft of the periscope lay waiting in its circular well while the helmsman steered the U-boat by means of dual press-buttons. Aft of the helmsman were the diving coxswains who were in control of the hydroplanes.

Janine nudged me with an elbow.

"Let's go to your cabin, your majesty."

I muttered, "Sorry, lieutenant. I really ought to familiarize myself with the operational procedure of the boat."

I wandered from the control room through the engine room and the neat, compact galley where a couple of the mermaids were readying a lunch, through the engine room where the throb of the Diesels was deafening, into the chamber just aft of it, where the torpedo loading hatches and the compressors were visible.

Then I went forward past the control room to the captain's cabin, which was mine when I was aboard, through the wardroom and the petty officers' room into the forward torpedo room, and the crew's quarters.

To my surprise, four torpedos were stored on cradles, ready for use. When the merman in charge saw my upraised eyebrows, he grinned.

"Never can tell when some ship might detect us and try to drop a few cans."

"We're ready to fight, then?"

"At the first whisper of the alarm gong."

I did not know whether to be reassured or not.

I made my way back to my cabin. All this time Fleur had been right behind me. I told her I was going to lie down and rest, and that I was not to be disturbed.

I slept for eight hours, comfortably and without dreaming.

As I stretched under the covers upon awaking, I told myself that a couple more submarine rides like this, and I would be a new man. When I left the cabin, Fleur informed me that lunchtime and the dinner hour had come and gone. She had not permitted anybody to wake me.

"Good girl. You haven't eaten either, have you?"

She shook her head until her long yellow hair flew. I patted her rump—she jumped at my touch—and followed her to the galley. We feasted on sandwiches and coffee until Fleur started yawning.

It was close to midnight.

"Fleur, you can lie down for a rest in my cabin," I told her. "I have plans to make, so nobody'll bother you."

"I wish you'd bother me," she muttered.

I patted her bare thigh under the short military jacket she still affected. Her leg quivered to my touch. "Later, honey. Later," I more or less promised.

Fleur wanted me to come into the cabin while she undressed, but I told her I had things to do. We would not be raiding until later. Albania lies roughly three hundred and fifty miles from Thraxos. At a steady fifteen knots per hour, it would take the *Triton* only twenty hours to reach its destination. We had been under way for almost eighteen hours.

She agreed morosely that she did need some shut-eye.

I went to find Janine.

She was presiding over a meeting of ten mermen and fifteen mermaids. As I entered, they all came to their feet. I grinned and waved a hand.

"I may be king of the hill on Thraxos, but here I'm a tyro. Go on with what you were doing. I'll just listen."

Everything had been arranged. The *Triton* would be in the little harbor before Vlanditsa in two and a half hours. At three in the morning, the mermen and the mermaids would be crawling onto the quay to move off by groups of threes and fours for their prey. Each one had a tear gas container for indoor use.

"All we need is a few minutes," Janine pointed out. "We'll hit a number of houses, maybe even a young men's compound, if there is such a thing." Her face brightened at the idea. "Say, does anyone here know anything about Albania? Do they have places like a Y.M.C.A.?"

Nobody knew from nothing about Albania, except that it sided with the Red Chinese against the Russians over their ideological split.

"A political jail," I suggested suddenly. "They might have locked up a number of young college students who favor Russia."

153

"Even criminals would do," a mermaid murmured.

"No criminals," I commanded. "At least, not hardened ones."

"Young ones," simpered a mermaid, and everybody laughed.

Motors slowed, the *Triton* crept into the harbor. It did not surface. There was no need for that, the mer-people could swim underwater to the quay.

I reflected glumly that I had no chance to escape this way. I was no merman, I could scarcely go out with them and swim to shore. Or could I? There must be scuba equipment in the *Triton*.

I asked Janine about it.

"You want to go along?" she asked. There was a devilish glee in her green eyes.

"I'd like to, yes."

"Good! So would I. Come along, we'll go find out about the skin-diving gear."

I smothered my groan. I could scarcely abandon ship with the redhead at my elbow. I could not back down, however. I went with her to find air tanks, goggles and rubber fins for our feet, thinking about Ernst Bachmann's notebooks in my jacket pocket where they would have to stay.

We uncovered our scuba equipment in a locker inside the ward room. I suppose S.E.L.L. needed the gear for training purposes. We each selected an air tank and mouthpiece, flippers for our feet, and a black leather belt that held a knife. Janine was giggling, then she was telling me we had forgotten to bring swimsuits.

"I'll wear shorts," I chuckled.

"I'll wear panties," she nodded.

We dressed in my cabin. Janine wore one of my shirts as we strode into the galley—the escape hatch formed part of its ceiling—and joined the others. It was one minute to three. One of the mermen began the countdown. Then, one by one, the mermaids and the mermen clambered through the escape haatch and darted outward into the harbor waters.

Janine dropped my shirt, exposing her heavy white
154

breasts. She gurgled laughter when she saw me eyeing them. Her breasts shook lazily to her movements as she stepped up onto the metal ladder and began her climb. With my eyes on her jiggling white buttocks, only partially hidden by her bikini-type panties, I went after her.

The water was black. I caught a glimpse of bare white legs where Janine was swimming, then the water closed around me and I was following her beachward. I swam easily, breathing in the tanked air. The swim was little more than a hundred yards, and I felt healthy and ready to go when my hands brushed against the quaystones on the harbor bottom.

I surfaced and climbed up the quay, then turned to assist Janine. Her red hair was plastered to her head and shoulders, but her soft laughter was a crooning contentment as she realized my body was reacting to her near nakedness.

"Come on," she breathed, kicking off her rubber flippers. "We've got to join the others."

We ran on bare feet across the cool stones of the harbor quay, listening to the faint sounds that told where the merpeople were at their tasks of kidnapping. A woman screamed, then was silent. I heard a male voice cry out. A door opened and slammed.

Janine and I were running up a narrow street between old houses. Ahead of us a line of young men, some in pajamas, some naked but for their trousers. Their hands were tied at their wrists behind their backs, and they were attached to a long rope. Each youth was gagged so he could not cry out.

I am certain these Albanian young men though it was some kind of Communist raid being made on their village. Their faces were frightened, puzzled, as their eyes touched the merman who was leading them by the rope toward the quay. I counted seven before they moved on out of sight.

Janine was framed in the doorway of a house. Her hand waved at me. I moved toward her. I had never broken into a house before; not to abduct a young man, at any rate. I wondered how we would go about it.

Janine was fumbling at the lock. It was the old-fashioned kind that a hairpin could open if properly applied. Janine had a length of celluloid in her hand. In a moment the door swung wide upon the darkness. Janine moved inside with me at her pink heels.

There was the smell of cookery in the front room. With the moonlight shining in the big bay window, we could make out heavy furniture, and in the background, a stairway with a lattice-work balustrade. Janine leaped for the railing.

Upstairs there were four bedrooms. In one room, two young men about eighteen and nineteen were sound asleep. Janine lifted out her knife, nodding her head at me. The touch of cold steel at two throats woke the youths from their slumbers.

Their eyes bulged. Their mouths opened.

When the knifepoints bit in, they closed their mouths. Janine breathed, "Not a sound, you understand? Or we'll slit your throats!"

Fear showed in their faces. Janine chuckled. She tore a strip from a sheet and gagged each man. Her flashing knife told them to get on their feet. I tied their hands behind them. I pushed them out into the hall.

There was another young man in the second room. In three minutes he was standing beside the others. In the third room a little girl lay sleeping. Janine closed the bedroom door softly. In the fourth room there was an older man, with a woman: evidently the father and mother.

Janine closed the door. I urged the three men down the stairs and out onto the street. We pointed at the quay. The young men began to trot.

When we arrived at the harbor, we found a dinghy filled with youthful male prisoners. Janine whispered that our captives were to join the others. As they got in, the gag of one of them came loose. Looking at Janine, he muttered something.

"What did he say?" I asked.

"He said, 'First blood to the Russkys, but the Red Chinese have yet to be heard from.' " Her giggle was quite mirthful. "They think we're Moscow agents. Good, let them think it."

The captives were made to ship oars and begin rowing.

156

The night air was cool, and my wet flesh shivered to the bite of the sea wind. I saw Janine was shaking, so I put an arm about her and drew her against me. She nestled there contentedly.

As the submarine surfaced, the captives were told to step out onto its deck still awash with water. One by one they mounted the conning tower steps, then climbed down the ladder into the kiosk. We followed them at the double, even as the order to submerge was being given.

Nobody wanted to stay out in the open like this, even if there was no heavy artillery in the little fishing village. If we were not seen, the mystery of the disappearance of so many young males would be even greater.

There was something like a chaotic mob scene in the control room as the mermaids began grabbing the prisoners, fondling and kissing them. My Amazons figured they had restrained themselves long enough. They were practically stripping the youths down, right here and now.

The mermen were looking on jealously, their faces dark and angrily flushed. A couple of them stood with twitching fingers as if they would reach out and grab some of the prey away from the female members of their undersea fellowship.

I began to realize that the change of hormones in the mermen was working at full speed now. They were no longer able to restrain the feminine characteristics in their bodies. They wanted a piece of the action with the prisoners.

I moved forward with Janine at my left elbow. To my surprise, Fleur was also there to lend a hand.

"Break it up. Get to your quarters! Snap it up!"

There were fifteen mermaids, and about thirty young prisoners. Each mermaid grabbed a man and dragged him with her. The others stood dazed, looking as if each man thought himself in the middle of a nightmare.

One or two of the merman began making advances to the remaining males, who stared at them in something akin to horror. As commander of this little expedition, I had to keep order. I dared not risk mutiny or at best, a pitched battle in these confined quarters.

"All right, you mermen! Go ahead!"

The mermen whooped with delight. They fastened upon the smaller, slimmer prisoners and dragged them after them to their quarters. The few who were left, I put in the ward room under guard by Fleur.

Janine and I and a skimpy complement of three mermen, who handled the controls, were left. I motioned Janine to take the main switches. I posted myself at the helm. I told the other mermen they would get their chance, but that they had to handle the *Triton* right now. They were sensible about it.

We proceeded at a speed of five knots past the Ionian islands. Before we reached the Gulf of Kiparissia, the mermen began straggling back to their posts, looking sheepish but satisfied. I released the mermen who had been handling the controls, letting them in on the fun.

Very faintly I could hear faint cries and shouts, feminine squeals and screeches. When the helmsman returned, grinning abashedly, I turned the helm over to his experienced hands and proceeded forward.

In the ward room I found a scowling Fleur, staring vacantly into space, and five glum prisoners seated on the floor. Fleur flashed me a disgusted glance and looked away. I think she had tried to get the prisoners to manhandle her and so activate her masochistic instincts, but they had suspected a trick and were leaving her strictly alone. I brushed past her, delivering a whack of my palm to her backside. She jerked and managed a faint smile.

In an old U-boat such as this, the crew's headquarters were bunks in the torpedo room. I stared in at those bunks filled with naked bodies squirming and moving, making throaty, passionate sounds. I saw a male rump bobbing up and down at furious speed, I noted a quivering white female thigh lifted sideways, I saw one girl with her head dangling over the edge of the bunk, eyes closed and tongue moving around her kiss-swollen lips. I paused to survey a feminine backside half over the bunk's edge, steadily jerking.

I sighed in sympathy with this love-in.

Fortunately I had never been so starved as this, but then,

158

my body had not been shot through with sea-serum and high level radiation. When you begin fooling around with the human body, medically speaking, sometimes you get odd results. These mermaids had become nymphomaniacs, constantly needing sexual satisfaction, yet never quite achieving it.

The mermen were luckier. They had just had their bill of fare changed on them. Instead of girls, they went for boys. But at least, they could get their fill of sex for a little while. The mermaids never could.

In the petty officers' room I discovered four of the mermaids with four naked Albanians. They were involved in a kind of daisy chain of bodies, so that they made a rough circle. I studied their contortions with the practiced eyes of a professional sexologist.

My Egyptian charmer was kneeling over a slim youth, head bobbing; the head of her victim was buried between the thighs of a slim blonde girl who was, in turn, adoring the manhood of a second Albanian, who was devoting himself to a third mermaid crouched above his face, and so on.

The Egyptian lifted her head and gave a hoarse shout.

She got to her feet, bending forward with her hands on her knees, legs spread wide. Her lover thrust into her in the ram manner of the Hindus. Each of the other four couples played follow the leader. They went at it that way, with the women screaming thickly as male hands caught and played with their dangling breasts, their hips lifting and dropping or swinging from side to side.

I sighed. They had been at this play a long time. I wondered what other designs for venery my inventive Egyptian had come up with. I made a mental note to ask her; I enjoy gleaning information for my League of Sexual Dynamics wherever it is to be found.

I moved aft toward the control room.

My cabin door was open. Janine was in there, a naked male between her wide-flung thighs, lifting and dropping. Apparently my second-in-command could not wait for me to assuage the fires of her lust. I closed the door on them very gently.

Through the Gulf of Kiparissia and into the Sea of Crete

159

we traveled, then the helm swung to take us north by northwest toward Thraxos. I busied myself through much of this time by arranging a diet for our male prisoners. If they were going to serve as studs, they must be ready, willing and able to perform their duties.

The proper food, a goodly amount of exercise—outdoors and in the open air and sunlight, running, jumping and leaping; no daytime bed calisthenics—and they would be ready, come every evening, to fulfill their diddling duties. I really felt like a king caring for his subjects, working on this project.

I was almost tempted to forget my obligations to Walrus-moustache for a while, just to see how this thing turned out. But I knew I could never do that. Besides, I had to go back to my job at the university, come the fall semester.

I had failed in my attempt to escape with Ernst Bachmann's notebooks explaining the sea-serum and the radiation treatments. I would have to dream up another escape, and next time, make it stick.

When we landed at Thraxos, everybody not held incommunicado—like Ernst Bachmann—was down at the marina to meet us. Those women who were not mermaids pounced on the ten untried males and began drawing them toward their rooms. The mermaids put up a squawk at that, because they wanted to sample those other boys, but I told them it was share and share alike, and that they had to be satisfied with that arrangement for the time being. They gave me some dirty looks, but they obeyed.

I had called a halt to the mermaid operations. I figured that with the sea-girls we already had, our complement was large enough. If I made any more of them, we would be spending all our time kidnapping male studs to keep them happy; and I had other ideas.

I realized now I would never be able to escape from Thraxos via submarine. Other methods of locomotion were indicated. A fishing smack, perhaps, or a shallop I could row. It would be a long, hard row; my best bet was some sort of boat with a sail.

All this would take time.

160

And so I resigned myself to a steady day-after-day diet of planning mermen and mermaid raids on yachts and small vessels plying the waters of the Aegean Sea. The mer-people were fantastically successful. They were fast making us wealthy.

Every hour I expected to see a flight of Greek or Turkish warplanes overhead, searching us out. We were pirates, and every nation whose shipping suffered from our depredations would be hunting for our lair.

The trouble came, however, from a completely different source.

CHAPTER TEN

Fleur was almost hysterical.

She had followed me into my quarters in the compound after dinner, disregarding my remark that I wanted to get some sleep. In the short military jacket that showed off her slim, tanned legs and the lace edges of her scant panties, she was sexually attractive; I admit that much. But I was determined that Fleur would be a masochist no longer.

I hoped, by my treatment, to make her understand that she would get no satisfaction from me as long as she went on needing pain before she could get her pleasure. My prescription was working. I could see that. She was desperate for any kind of sexual relief.

She stood there, berating me as I turned on the little bed lamp. "You never give me any of your time," she panted, her blue eyes filled with tears. "Damn you, I need fun too. You take care of those hot-pants mermaids and the mermen by getting them studs! But you won't even look at me!"

"Fleur, take it easy," I murmured.

"I will not take it easy!" she screamed.

She was sobbing, hands working, tears streaming down her cheeks. For a moment I thought she was going to leap on me and attempt a rape, but her quivering fingers went to the buttons of her khaki tunic. They blurred as she unfastened those metal discs and threw open the flaps.

Her breasts were hard and swollen, and the red nipples were elongated a full inch. Fleur Devot had the longest nipples I have ever seen on a woman. They were hard and thick, and their color was an angry scarlet.

She advanced, jutting her breasts at me.

162

"You see? I'm as much a woman as any of those sluts you've been banging. I need it too."

"There are prisoners you could——"

She swung at my face with a pink palm. I caught her hand, yanking her up against me. I asked brutally, "How do you want it?"

"You k-know!" she yelled. "What you call Venus aversa!"

I shook my head. "You just want pain. There's more to male and female relationships than some kink you're hung up on. Forget the pain. Enjoy yourself with a normal kind of relationship."

She drew a gurgling breath between a laugh and a sob. "All right. Any way at all! I'm too far gone to care about methods now."

She bent to push her panties down her plump little hips.

Outside, a gunshot sounded. And another.

She froze like that, eyes wide, staring up at me while my eyes, that had been riveted to her lower belly, swiveled toward the door. There was another gunshot and somebody screamed.

"What is it?" Fleur whimpered.

I thought about a raid by Greek or Turkish troops. They had found the pirate lair and were attacking. The irony of the situation touched a bitter nerve in me. I had hoped for some such action, but it was far too premature. I myself would be caught as the ringleader of the attackers, and even Walrus-moustache would not be able to help me.

I reached for my Luger and clicked off the light in practically the same movement. I crept toward the door. My hand reached for the knob as Fleur spoke.

"What about me?" she whimpered.

"Are you putting me on?" I snarled. "Listen to those gunshots! We're under attack. And at a time like this, you want to play games?"

She sobbed. I opened the door and stepped out.

A running man across the compound held an automatic rifle in a hand. He was not a merman; he was wearing our uniform for the Albanian prisoners. I saw him turn at sight of me and raise his rifle.

I held the Luger on him, squeezing its trigger. His body went backward as if he had been kicked by a giant hoof. He hit the ground and lay still.

Hearing footsteps, I whirled, smoking automatic raised to fire again. A merman raced around the corner. He raised his hand, palm forward.

"Hold it, your majesty! It isn't us mermen—it's the Albanians who are rebelling!"

"The Albanians?" I gasped in amazement.

The prisoners had appeared quite satisfied with their lot up until now. They were well fed; they were looked after like young princes; and all they had to do was go to bed with some overanxious females.

"They want their freedom do they?" I snarled.

"It's more than that. They want the secret of how to make mermen and mer-girls. They have Ernst Bachmann as a hostage. They intend to take him back with them to Albania."

"But why, for God's sake?"

The merman growled, "They want to hand over his secrets to the Red Chinese. The Albanians have allied themselves with the Maoists, you know."

I thought about the Red Chinese with their millions of slave-labor males. They could make an army of a million mermen without any trouble. Then they could unleash that array of mermen killers on the Pacific coast of the United States.

The mere thought of a million confirmed believers in Mao Tse-tung clambering out of the Pacific Ocean armed with automatic rifles, hand grenades and grenade launchers, maybe even with tanks, made me shudder. At all costs, I had to stop this fiasco!

I ran at top speed toward the marina.

I yelled at the mermen to get the women, to rouse up the other mermen. I angled my run past the Albanian I had shot, grabbing his automatic rifle and a bandolier that held bullets for the gun.

The night was dark, there was just a cusp of moon in the sky. Ahead of me I could make out a few dim figures racing toward the marina. Apparently their attack had been

164

planned a long time. While some of them kept the mermen and the mermaids and the other women busy at their sex games, these others would pounce on Ernst Bachmann and make a beeline for the *Triton*. I didn't know how they expected to launch it; I felt positive none of them had ever been aboard an underseas craft before. Maybe they planned to take along those mermen who did.

One of them turned at the sound of my pounding footsteps. I saw a rifle come up. I dropped flat on the ground.

With the wooden stock against my cheek, I fired a blast into those shadowy figures. Four of them went down, including the man who had turned to fire at me.

Behind me I could hear screams of fright and an occasional gunshot. My blood ran cold as sweat dripped down my face. Suppose the Albanians with the girls and the mermen had hidden revolvers somewhere close by and were now using them? Unarmed, even naked for their sex-play, the Amazons and the mermen would fall easy victims to the sneak attack.

I dared not turn. I had to stop the prisoners ahead of me from reaching the *Triton*. I ran on through the cool night.

To my surprise, the Albanians bypassed the pathway that lead to the marina where the *Triton* lay docked. They were moving on toward the steps built to take the members of this S.E.L.L. compound to the beach. I ran after them as fast as I could pump my feet.

Once I saw two of them outlined against the sky. I heaved the automatic rifle to my shoulder and let go a burst. Both men dropped, bodies jerking as those lead slugs ploughed into them.

I got to the top of the wooden staircase in time to see a dinghy drawn up on the beach, mast stepped in place, big sail rippling with the seawind sweeping across the Aegean from the Greek mainland. There were a dozen men down there. One of them had his arms tied behind his back. Ernst Bachmann.

I rested the barrel of the Russian-made AK-47 on a stair rail and steadied it. I peered down at the men about to enter the boat.

My finger squeezed the trigger. The automatic rifle bucked against my shoulder, again and again. I saw the Albanians dropping like flies on the sand. Then one of them yanked out a gun and aimed it at Ernst Bachmann.

"Stop—or I kill him!" he screamed.

If I had been a S.E.L.L. operative, or even if I had wanted really to create a pirate empire here on Thraxos, I might have obeyed that hysterical command. I was neither. I took a better aim and let go.

Bullets spattered the sand until they zeroed in on the man with the revolver. But by the time his body jerked and shuddered to half a dozen lead pellets ripping through his flesh, he had fired his own gun. At Bachmann.

The biochemist reeled, staggering in the sand. His body was upright, so for one wild moment I thought maybe the man had missed. Then the German started to topple forward. He lay there face down on the pebbly beach and never moved again.

I ran down the stairs.

Kicking sand at every footfall, I went to body after body, testing each for any signs of life. There were none. Every man lying there prone on the sand was dead. I grabbed their weapons and tossed them, with their supply of ammunition, into the boat.

Then I turned and raced for the stairs.

I was panting when I reached the top. The cliffs on this side of the island are high and straight, and I had not paused to count steps. I got my second wind, then raced toward the buildings in the distance, where the sound of gunshots told me the mermen and my Amazons were putting up a hard fight against the Red-Chinese-oriented Albanians.

My hands inserted a new clip into the rifle as I ran. From the sounds I heard as I approached, I realized the women's quarters had been turned into a battleground.

I sped past the unmoving body of a merman and, ten feet further on, that of a dead Albanian. I ran up to a broken window and peered inside.

The backs of seven Albanians were turned to me as they fired across the dormitory at some of the women who had

166

put up a couple of mattresses as a bulwark. The mattresses were hanging in shreds. I spotted ten dead women, lying face down or face up as death had caught them.

My AK-47 barrel slid through the busted window.

I hit the trigger. A spray of bullets ran from the automatic rifle into the backs of the Albanians. From left to right and back again from right to left I raked them. They were standing, dead on their feet, bodies still moving as my hail of lead rammed into them.

When they collapsed, I yelled to the girls.

"You can come out now! They're dead."

Celeste Maillot poked her blonde head between the mattresses. "That you, Damon?"

One by one, they stood up—all four of them. The others were lying dead on the far side of the upright mattresses. Four left, out of more than twenty! I went in the door and walked toward the survivors.

"They caught us by surprise," Celeste muttered. "Just when we were all about to trade lovers, and the men were going from one bed to the other, they grabbed their guns."

"Luckily we'd turned out the lights, for kicks," a Grecian brunette murmured, sobbing. "We thought it would be more fun that way—not knowing which of them was balling us."

"It saved our lives, I guess," Celeste added. "They couldn't see too well in the darkness. They missed a lot more than they hit. We grabbed up mattresses and our weapons, and began shooting back after turning on the lights so we could see what the hell we were doing."

"All right, come on. We have more of them to flush out."

The mermen in their quarters would have been caught the same way by the Albanians who serviced them. My four remaining girl friends fell into step on either side of me.

The mermen's quarters were dark.

The hairs on the back of my neck stood up. I smelled deathtrap. I put out an arm, halting the girls.

"Take cover," I whispered.

167

I stayed there alone, waiting until my Amazons were behind buildings. Then I shouted.

"You in there—answer me!"

The answer was a hail of lead from three windows. I dropped flat and began my crawl across the compound. As if we had practiced it, my four girls slid into view on their bellies, cradling their own weapons to their shoulders. They pumped lead into those windows as a covering fire until I got myself behind a building wall.

There was a woman there. Fleur.

"Where'd you come from?"

"When you ran after the Albanians, I ran to find the other girls. I g-got scared, so I turned and ran after you. But then I heard the sounds of shooting in the merman quarters. I froze, I guess."

"You unfrozen?"

"I g-guess so."

"Then get me some grenades and a launcher. And step on it, baby. We've got to cool it in there."

She ran, military jacket flapping above her pantied behind.

"You inside there," I bellowed at the Albanians. "The rest of your fellows are dead. You're all alone. You'll be dead in a little while too, unless you surrender."

Soft curses were my answer.

Fleur ran up, staggering under the weight of an M-17 grenade launcher. I grabbed it, rammed a grenade down its maw and set the stock to my shoulder. My finger hit the trigger. There was a whoosh—and about a second later red flame blew up inside the mermen's quarters. I could see bits of bodies flying all around inside that scarlet hell.

There was silence. I got up and moved forward with my girls all around me. We put our heads inside the window and withdrew them. There was nobody alive inside that shattered building.

"All right, girls—scatter! See if you can find anybody else around who's alive."

I set off toward my own quarters. All I needed was the packet containing Ernst Bachmann's notebooks. When it made a good weight in my hand, I beat feet for the beach

168

and the dinghy the Albanians had intended to make their escape in. It was there, surrounded by dead bodies.

I put my hands to the curved prow and pushed.

The dinghy did not move. Then two hands slammed against the prow beside my own. I looked at Fleur Devot, pale and determined.

"Come on, push!" she panted. "The time I'm going to have you all to myself, dammit!"

We pushed. The dinghy slid an inch, two inches. Then the water was under its keel and the going was easier. I was tempted to tell Fleur to go back to the other girls, but my common sense told me that was one order she would not obey.

Besides, I had a plan for Fleur.

When the dinghy was two feet out from shore, Fleur swung herself over the moldboard. I followed her an instant later. To my surprise she went to the sail, began running it up the mast. I moved aft to the rudder, glancing at the blonde in surprise.

"You know how to sail?"

"I was born on the coast of Brittany," she answered.

The wind blew strong, and within minutes we were cleaving the blue waters of the Aegean toward the Greek mainland. Fleur was very quiet, glancing at me from time to time.

Finally she said, "You took something from your room, didn't you? Those notebooks." She smiled when she saw my cautious glance. "Oh, I knew a long time ago you weren't just a professor."

"Okay, I took Bachmann's notebooks. Bachmann's dead. Nobody's going to make men into mermen again if the Thaddeus X. Coxe Foundation can help it."

"Good," she nodded. "I'm glad."

A Greek naval patrol boat picked us up twenty hours out of Thraxos. We were fed and taken to the American embassy in Athens. There I issued a statement to the Greek naval officer in command at their base, telling them that the pirate lair was a thing of the past, but that they could recover all the loot that had been stolen by sending a couple of vessels there.

A plane carried Fleur and me to Marseilles. From Marseilles, we went by helicopter to St. Tropez. I was wondering how I was going to explain Fleur to the baroness. I need not have worried. The baroness was in Paris, shopping for fall clothes.

Walrus-moustache was still in St. Tropez, however.

He looked tanned and healthy, and, for him, was very grateful for my efforts. His hands went over the notebooks as if they were a woman.

"It's too bad, but I'll have to destroy them. Orders from on high," he told me, seated in a chair on the beach where Fleur, in a black bikini bottom and a couple of pasties over her nipples, was walking into the water. I drew my eyes from her twitching buttocks to stare at him.

"You mean after all I went through you're going to *burn* them? I could have done that myself, first night I was on that island."

"I'm sure you'd have missed a lot of fun if you had," he chuckled, and glanced at Fleur where she was diving into the blue Mediterranean. Since only *le minimum* strings were visible from behind, it seemed that she was stark naked.

I opened my mouth to protest. I closed it.

Maybe he had something there.

I relaxed in the hot sun, thinking about Fleur and her problem. I felt that my case was incomplete unless I did something about her hang-up. How to go about it? How best to teach her that pain need not be the trigger to fire off her passion? I settled back in the sunlight and thought.

And so, that evening, as I walked with Fleur Devot to her room in the Hotel de la Tour, I carried a few odds and ends in my pockets. She looked eatable in a black satin evening gown, out of which her bare shoulders and half of her breasts rose proudly. The cloth molded itself to the full buttocks quivering to her stride, naked under the satin. Her shapely legs were contained in silvered stockings.

We had just come from the Diabolique, and we walked in a swirl of heated flesh and prickling passion. Fleur seemed almost in a daze. I guess she had never seen anything quite like that stage show and the carryings-on of the

170

people in the audience. I had deliberately refrained from touching her. I wanted her simmering, like a pot on a stove.

She was simmering just right. As I inserted the key in the lock of her door, she was rubbing her thighs together and making little moaning sounds. When I pushed open the door, I put a hand on her buttocks and urged her into darkness.

"Don't turn on the light," I murmured.

I closed the door and locked it. From my pocket I brought out a sleeping mask, one of those black cloth pads attached to a rubber band. I fitted it over her head. When she exclaimed in surprise, I kissed her pouting lips.

"You aren't Fleur Devot any longer," I told her. "You're just a woman. Any woman. You have only two senses left to you, those of taste and touch. This is the last word you will hear from me for some time to come."

I pushed twin earplugs into her ears and so that I could experience this same loss of identification, I slipped a mask over my eyes and placed plugs in my own ears, as well. Instantly I felt alone, abandoned in a black emptiness that was almost terrifying in its completeness.

I put out a hand, as if to seek human companionship. I touched Fleur on her bare arm. I pulled her closer, bent my head and kissed up that arm to her shoulder. She was shaking; I knew that much. I could neither see nor hear her, but suddenly I could feel her hand touch my middle and move downward.

Her fingers clutched my rigid manhood.

I slid her shoulder strap down. I could not see her, I could not hear her, so I used my lips across the shoulder I had bared to search out and discover the nakedness of her flesh. I licked her flesh hungrily as I pushed the panel of her gown off her breast.

My tongue learned the shape of that rockhard breast, the pebbled contour of the rubbery nipple. I took it into my mouth, I suckled at it, I used my tongue to whip it as I might a candy. Fleur was pressing her bared breast into my face, trying to move it from side to side. It felt like a big balloon.

My hands slipped across her bare back and down to her
171

hips. My tactile sense was sharply heightened by my isolation from sight and sound. Her back was like whipped cream to the touch. Her other shoulder strap had come down by this time, I felt her palms catch my cheeks and draw my mouth to her neglected nipple.

Just touch and taste.

I slid my open mouth down her front, away from her swollen breasts. I kissed her navel, let my tongue-tip know its contours. My mouth went across the faint bulge of her belly that moved against my face as she panted. By slipping downward, I had dragged myself from her clutching hand. She must have been angry, her hands twisted themselves in my hair and shook my head from side to side.

While she was doing that, my hands were yanking her black satin evening gown down past her hips. My hands followed the gown past her fleshy hips and along her smooth thighs to the tops of her silvered stockings. I caressed her warm flesh, feeling her thighs rubbing together and her hips swinging in a rotary motion.

Her hands were under my face, trying to convey the idea she wanted me to stand. I got to my feet and found that her own hands wanted in on the action. Fleur undid my tie, unbuttoned my shirt, freed my belt with thumbs and forefingers, and made my pants slide down. I obliged her by stepping out of my shorts.

Naked, I felt her own naked body come against mine. She used her belly, her breasts and her thighs to caress me. She slid around on me, back and forth, all soft flesh against which my manhood brushed and bumped. Fleur turned her body all around, moving it against me so I could sense its softness, its heat. When her buttocks touched my extended flesh, they became gentle, lifting and falling and arching as though she wanted to learn my shape through that one area alone.

I took advantage of her position to put my hands around her waist, to caress her belly, to slide fingertips down across her shaven privacy. The movements of her behind became more abandoned. When my fingertip sought out her twig, she mashed her buttock cheeks into me and shook.

172

I could not hear her panting, but I am certain she was, because my own lungs were going in and out like a bellows. I did not feel like Rod Damon any longer; I was merely Man. Fleur was only Woman. No longer Fleur Devot, no more a French starlet, but just a Female playing with a nameless Male.

I could only hope this therapeutic treatment was working. My little blonde starlet was discovering that her body reacted to gentle caresses, to a slow build-up of fondlings and kisses, to touch and taste. She did not need pain to get a glow on. In the dark silence enveloping us both, she was almost a virgin learning about sex for the first time.

I kissed her bare shoulder. I ran my tongue down her spine. My fingernails scratched lightly along her sides, all the way to her hips. My lips kissed her quivering buttocks, my tongue tasted them. Fleur stood trembling, accepting this adoration of her unclad loveliness. She was not thinking of pain now. Only of the pleasure I was showering upon her flesh.

I kissed her thighs, her knees, her calves. I devoted myself to her nakedness as if I must learn her beauty by touch of tongue and lips alone. She understood what I was trying to accomplish, I am positive. She turned her naked body this way and that, adding to its pleasure by partaking of it.

And then—she was gone.

My arms held no longer her naked hips, her buttock cheeks were no longer warm beneath my mouth. I gave a shocked cry, not realizing she could not hear me.

A hand touched my bare back, moved down blindly to my own buttocks, slid around in front to where I strained for pleasure. The hand was smooth and warm; it was my entire world at that moment. It took my flesh into a cupped hand. Another hand came to join it, discovering shape and size and hardness.

Sensing that this intimate investigation was an integral part of my plan to free her from her former slavery to pain, I tried to remain as detached as possible. I let those hands probe and stroke and weigh. My body was shaking uncontrollably, however. Despite my experience as a practicing sexologist, I was also a man.

Her mouth came to join her hands in their explorations. I gave a cry, I fell backwards at the touch of her tongue and her soft, moist lips. I lay there shaking, realizing she was as blind and deaf as I, and that she was using the only method left to her to know my body better.

Her lips closed on me, holding me.

Gently my hips thrust upward. She seemed to understand, she worked slowly and gently, all over me until she knew my form as a sculptor knows his clay. Then her head moved faster. The pleasure she gave me was excrutiatingly pleasant. I had no sight nor sound to distract my attention. I lived only at that point of my greatest excitation. The world had nothing else in it for me at the moment.

Then my hand reached out and ran down a shaking thigh. I caressed the soft flesh, I hooked her thigh and drew it closer so that her knees slid upon the carpet. I lifted her thigh, drew it over me. I could not see it, my caressing hands molded it so in my mind I sensed its quivering, its widespread stance. My hands slid on up across her haunches. My fingers fastened in her shaking buttocks.

I drew her downward and explored her womanhood with my mouth and tongue, as she was doing to me. I could not hear her, the only means I had to determine how I was affecting her was the movement of her teeth and mouth. Those teeth bit and scraped; the lips soothed and caressed.

For an eternity of ecstasy, we floated in blackness.

Fleur rippled and shook, again and again. Her body leaped and danced above my own as sensations to which she had been alien exploded through her flesh. A cathartic carnality held her in its grip. She was a different woman now. The mere brush of her rock-hard breasts across my belly told me that pleasure and not pain would be the guidepost for her conduct from now on.

My hands gripped her haunches, pushing them sideways. She rolled and I went with her, but now I was sliding about so my face was above her own. My fingers went to her mask, sliding it loose as I lifted off my own. I removed our earplugs.

174

"Ohhhh," she moaned, hips lifting.

My eyes stared down into her delight-contorted face as I moved into her body. She welcomed me, arms clasped about me. Her hips slowly picked up the beat and began pounding against the floor. To cushion her softness, I gripped her with my hands, lifting her, directing her movements.

She screamed three times in two minutes.

When I slowed and withdrew, Fleur Devot was staring at the ceiling with a wild, bright light in her face. "Why didn't someone tell me?" she whispered. "Why, Rod? I never realized. I never properly understood!"

"And maybe you never would have if I hadn't settled on this mode of treatment. You'd have laughed at me if I suggested anything different from what's always given you your kicks."

Her laugh was roguish. "Maybe I would," she admitted, lifting her arms to fold them about my neck so she could kiss me with open mouth. "Who knows the way of a maid?"

I do, I wanted to tell her. But maybe she sensed that, because she drew away her mouth long enough to say, "How about another lesson, Professor?"

Somehow, I got the feeling she might become my star pupil, given enough time. And I had plenty of time. I wasn't due back at the university for another couple of weeks.

The second lesson started coming up.